HOME FROM HOME

a novel by Roy W. Taylor

R. W. Taylor

First published in August 2015.

BOOK ONE : SEPTEMBER 1971

1

As she approached the entrance to the market, Rose observed that the two flower ladies were mounting guard as usual on either side of the opening. In response to their pleadings, she shook her head and passed on. She liked to decorate her small flat with flowers. With each chrysanthemum costing the equivalent of little more than a penny in the new UK coinage it was a luxury which a missionary on even a very basic allowance like hers could afford; but no matter how many you bought, these women would urge you to buy more. It was hard to see how they could make much of a profit, however, despite their sales pitch.

The vegetable woman greeted her like a long-lost friend and immediately began to hold up various mysterious items for her inspection. In her best Taiwanese she asked for carrots and potatoes, even though the woman appeared to consider that these were not exotic enough for her; and, having resisted the woman's attempt to add an extra potato in order to make it up to a round sum, paid her money and left.

She had got used to these markets by now. Ten years earlier, when she had first arrived, the great variety of smells (some of them distinctly unpleasant), the sides of pork hanging up without the protection of a refrigerator, the tanks of fish swimming in circles and blissfully unaware of their impending fate and the motor bikes that threaded their way relentlessly between the stalls might have unnerved her, but now they were a part of normal life, even thought they were very different from the recently reconstructed market in her native Blackburn.

For her this market was very conveniently placed. A two minute walk down Victory Road brought her to the tall iron gates of the school where she lived and worked. "Nancheng Presbyterian Bible College" read the battered old notice, which she had long thought ought to be replaced, or, at the very least, touched up, to give a better impression.

As she passed the porter's lodge, she observed old Tan lying asleep on his tatami mattress, undeterred by the odd fly buzzing round his nostrils. She turned right, passing some classrooms, and left again, thus bringing her to the girls' dormitory, of which she was warden. The building was constructed on the four sides of a central courtyard, an arrangement which was meant to ensure cooling breezes in the summer heat. Even so, her room could be unbearably hot.

She let herself in with her key. Other members of staff had more spacious accommodation, whereas, having only a year earlier been moved here from other work, she had to be content with a room no bigger than the study bedrooms which housed those few girls fortunate enough to live alone. Although she did not complain outwardly, she found this lack of space very constricting: she liked to entertain friends, but if she had more than three guests there was hardly room for anyone to move.

One thing that pleased her, however, was that she had been given the freedom to decorate it in such a way as to give it some individual character. Her walls were painted pastel blue, in contrast with the plain white of other rooms, and hanging prominently there was a picture of Pendle Hill, which she had taken herself many years before with her Brownie Box and had had enlarged at a local shop. The curtains she had made herself with material purchased at the cloth market after a whole afternoon of comparing stall with stall and haggling for good prices: the red tulips against a pale blue background provided welcome splashes of colour. The bookshelves attached to the wall housed a few devotional books, some Bible commentaries, some missionary biographies, some Agatha Christie novels and a few miscellaneous works. On her desk stood a photograph of her parents taken on holiday in Blackpool: the knotted handkerchief on her father's head was his particular protection when the sun was strong. Another photograph depicted her younger sister, Ethel, with her husband and baby Simon, taken two years earlier, just after the happy event. The large rocking chair, which dominated the room, she had bought soon after her arrival in Taiwan: here she could rock herself steadily as she prayed for friends or simply rest her eyes after some busy work. A curtained recess contained her bed and a washbowl. For Rose Littleton, this was 'home'.

According to Chinese custom, however, it was unthinkable to describe the quarters of a single person as 'home'. The word referred to those who were married, preferably with children. In the Chinese concept, the wider family also was important, with grandma exercising a bigger influence on the rest of her family than would have been permitted her in Britain. Sometimes Rose was painfully conscious that, as a single girl of 32, she was regarded by the Chinese as an oddity.

She looked at her watch. There was still time to correct a few English test papers before lunch. As she took out her red felt-tip pen, there was a loud knock on the door, and a voice cried : "Li Lausu! 'Li Lausu!"

Wondering what could have prompted such a desperate summons, Rose sprang to the door and opened it. Standing before her was Grace, one of the girls from the hostel. Each of the girls had been given an English name, and 'Grace' was one of the favourites. Addressing her teacher, she said, "Li Lausu! Please come quickly." She spoke in Taiwanese, a language which Rose now knew well. It had been hard at first, but by this time she was reasonably fluent. Although the government wanted everyone to use Mandarin, for many this was their heart language.

"What's the matter?" she asked.

"There's been an accident."

Horrible visions of mangled remains beneath the wheels of a bus came to mind. "An accident? Where?"

"The stairs. Florence." It was a relief to know that the city buses had not claimed another victim, but a fall downstairs, especially when they were made of concrete, could be a serious business. She pictured Florence lying inert on the concrete floor with an ugly swelling on her head, perhaps even with a gashed skull, still resting in a pool of blood, and made haste.

It was easy to see that something amiss had happened. A crowd of fellow students stood at the foot of the stairs, looking downwards in alarm and wearing an air of people facing events beyond their capacity to set right. Because of this crowd, it was not possible at first even to see Florence.

The arrival of their teacher was regarded with the sort of relief inspired by the arrival of the Mounties in a Western film, even though Rose's knowledge of First Aid was very limited.

As the throngs parted to let her through, she had her first glimpse of the victim, sitting on the floor, moaning and clutching her elbow. Her bosom friend, Catherine, was crouched down beside her with an arm round her shoulders.

"She fell downstairs," declared Catherine in case the teacher should not be aware of the circumstances

"You mean from the top to the bottom?" It must have been a serious fall to provoke such a reaction.

"Not all the way," Florence replied. The patient could speak. That was a good omen.

"What happened then?"

"It was only the last few steps; but I still hurt myself. I think my elbow is broken."

"Let me see." Watched carefully by the surrounding hordes – for numbers had grown – Rose gently took the arm of the sufferer. Although she had no medical training, the general consensus was that, because she was a foreigner, she must have the correct expertise. The conclusion she reached was that the arm seemed to be bruised rather than broken, and she announced this finding to the assembly. Then she addressed the patient: "Now why don't you get up?"

She extended a hand, and Florence took it with her good arm and allowed herself to be raised up. There was a stir of excitement from the onlookers, almost as if they had witnessed a biblical miracle.

"Let's go back to your room to rest a bit. If the pain persists, I suggest you go to see the college matron. We don't want to take any risks." As she led Florence away, the spectators, robbed of their quarry, broke up.

Rose tried to imagine this sort of thing happening in a British college. Their British counterparts would probably have demonstrated much more initiative. Yet she loved these girls, and was glad that she had the task of working amongst them.

2

"Just be patient, Sandy. It's nearly ready."

The dog was white, with two pale brown patches from which he got his name and two black ears and he was of no particular breed. An unwanted pet, he had been let loose in the seminary grounds, in the hope that someone would take pity on him. It had worked. Miss Alleyne Zimmer was now its proud owner.

At every mealtime he gave the impression that he had been starved for a month. "Here you are, you greedy boy," she remarked, as she tipped the contents of the pan into a bowl and set it on the stone floor. Even before the bowl reached its destination, the first mouthful was already consumed. As Sandy continued to devour the contents, the bowl slid along the floor until it came up against the wall. "You've no manners," she told him. "I suppose I ought to scold you for it, but it's gotten a bit late for that."

At 61, she had only four years to go until the end of her overseas service. She was aware that, with her greying hair, she looked her age, yet she still had plenty of energy. A member of that diminishing band of workers in Taiwan who had formerly served in Mainland China, she had been born there to missionary parents, who, in no way deterred by the aftermath of the Boxer Rebellion, had returned to work in that great country shortly before Sun Yat Sen's revolution, and thus she felt more Chinese than American.

On her walls were Chinese paintings mainly of mountains and rivers. One of these she particularly valued because it had been given to her parents by a mandarin. There were several wood carvings, which came from a village called San Yi here in Taiwan and marble artefacts given to her by grateful students. It was gratifying to think that she had been able to help so many young people during her years at the seminary. The furniture was mainly supplied by the college: it was old and rickety, but it served its purpose. After all, as a missionary, she had forsworn the very idea of luxury and ease. Her books were either Bible commentaries or missionary biographies of the old sort, from which all possible blemishes had been omitted. There was a Dorothy L. Sayers crime novel, which she had permitted herself to retain simply because this lady was also the author of good Christian books. On a coffee table was perched a pile of back copies of the 'Moody Monthly'.

"Finished already?" she questioned, with a lift of the eyebrows. "And you would take mine as well if I let you, wouldn't you?" Well, that's all you're getting, because your Aunty Alleyne knows what's good for you."

The dog gave a friendly wave of the tail, as if unaware of this criticism, and flopped down in his basket, ready to indulge in his second favourite occupation.

There was a timid knock on the door. "Come in !" she called. The door opened slowly. "Why, Ke-lin, do come in." This was Catherine's name in her own language.

"Sz Lausu, You wanted to see me?"

"Yes, I did. "I wanted to see you as soon as your main class was over. Why didn't you come then?"

"There was an accident. My friend, Florence – she fell down the stairs. I was trying to help her."

"Never mind. You're here now. Shut the door and take a seat."

Sandy gave a cautionary bark, which startled the visitor. "He won't hurt you," Miss Zimmer reassured her. " I wanted to see you because of your Old Testament report." Catherine shifted uneasily in her chair as if she sensed what was coming. "I have marked some bad reports in my time, but I find it hard to remember any that were worse than this one."

"I'm sorry," Catherine mumbled.

"How a girl in a seminary such as this could make so many mistakes in one short report I find it hard to imagine. You say that Israel was destroyed by Babylon, whereas it was Assyria."

Her visitor looked down. "I was confused. I know that really."

"It's obvious that you have not attended much to my lectures."

"It wasn't easy. I've had a lot of problems lately."

"What sort of problems?"

"My mother is in hospital. The bills are high. It's not even certain that I can afford to continue my studies. I get so worried about it."

At these words, Miss Zimmer softened her tone a little. "Have you told anyone else?"

"Only Florence."

"You haven't told any members of staff?"

"No, only you just now. I was too embarrassed."

"Embarrassed to talk with us? You know we are here to help you. I will mention this to the committee – if you don't object. They may be able to offer some financial assistance. We have bursaries."

"I would be grateful, Sz Lausu."

"I think they will be able to find a way to help you."

"Thank you, thank you, Sz Lausu."

Sandy wagged his tail as if to show that he too approved.

"So if you stop worrying about this, you may be able to produce good work for me again."

"Yes, Sz Lausu, I will do my best."

"Good. There goes the dinner bell. We'd better go and eat."

Miss Zimmer's room was on the ground floor of the hostel for single staff. Although the dining hall was just behind it, it was necessary to walk past the library to get there. She saw that new missionary coming out of the library. What was his name? Falconer, or something like that. She did not agree with the policy of letting outsiders borrow books from the library, so that when you wanted to borrow them yourself they were not available. He greeted her as he cycled past. She returned his greeting curtly as she continued on her way.

Apart from the refurbished library and the renovations to the boys' and girls' hostels, little had changed in the years she had been at the school. Numbers were higher than in the past, but this was probably because of the foolish policy of letting in those who could not gain entrance into any other educational establishment.

The dining hall was always too dark, especially by contrast when the sun was bright outside. She had suggested constructing more windows, but nobody had taken up the suggestion. The round tables and the stools would almost have qualified as antiques. Each table held seven. There was no separate table for staff, as it was expected they would mingle with the students.

A quick glance assured her that she was the only foreign member of staff on this occasion who condescended to eat with there. In the old days, missionaries were content to identify completely with their Chinese brethren; but missionaries these days thought too much about themselves. They would sit in their rooms drinking coffee and reading the latest magazine from home. She had talked about this with Gladys Aylward once on a visit to Taipei, shortly before her untimely death. At least she, Alleyne Zimmer, had never lowered her standards. She scooped rice into her mouth with her chopsticks.

3

As Peter Falconer cycled through the gateway of St. John's House, he glanced at his watch. 12.32: he was late for lunch. There were two buildings, both of them put up during the Japanese era. The smaller of the two contained his own living quarters – a kitchen, a bedroom, a study and a small living room, a room where church services where about to start for English speakers and a guest room. Instead of walls there were, for the most part, sliding doors, with netting on the ones that were on the outside of the house. The larger building housed 20 university students.

After placing his books temporarily on his study desk, he crossed the yard to the other building, which lay at right angles to his. The dining room was small and the cooking facilities restricted, yet old Su, the cook, managed to produce meals that were perfectly adequate for the needs of cash-strapped students. Seated at four tables, they had already started eating.

He took his place next to Mark, a thick-set youth now entering his fourth year, who grinned and produced a plate piled high with food. "We saved that for you," he declared in English .

Peter thanked him. It was far more than he really wanted, but he was grateful for the thought. He preferred to take his food from the common dishes like the rest of them; but he did not like to show ingratitude by putting the food back again.

"You finished your classes late?" Mark asked. He seized every opportunity to converse in English because he hoped to go abroad when he had graduated and completed his military service. It was a tradition in his family, and he did not want to be the odd one out.

"No, I called at the seminary to pick up some books. That's what made me late."

Mark left the table for a moment to stock up on extra rice. Another student, Bill, dressed for basketball, spoke to him in Mandarin: "You are always reading. I think you must have a lot of knowledge."

Peter said ruefully in Mandarin: " Reading makes you realize how little you really know."

"Don't be so modest," said a tall student called Wang Ming. (He did not like to use an English name.) "You went to Cambridge, didn't you?"

"It's still possible to go to Cambridge and yet be ignorant about a lot of things," Peter said. He could see, however, that they did not believe him. Here in Taiwan there was an exaggerated respect for graduates of Oxford and Cambridge.

"Cambridge graduates speak the best English," Mark declared, sporting a strong American accent. American influence was so strong here in this country, and many students went to the USA after graduation.

"Yours is the best kind of English," echoed Bill.

It was hardly an original conversation, but one which he had held many times with his students. It was the same with the students at the university to whom he taught English Literature. Although he had told them that they must form their own opinions, the normal Chinese respect for the teacher and the awe with which Cambridge graduates were regarded meant that, in exams, the few students he had taught in his spare time during language study in Taipei had tended to regurgitate the things he had told them rather than daring to put forward their own ideas. Perhaps he could make a better impression now that he was in full time lecturing.

The meal over, some students returned to their rooms for a siesta, some practised their basketball in the courtyard and others sat on the steps to talk. Peter sat with the latter group.

"You ought to get married, "said Wang Ming suddenly. He often spoke with a confident air, but when you got to know him better you realized that that this was hollow and there was a very immature person underneath.

Peter smiled. "Why do you say that?"

"You must be over 30."

"32."

"Then it's your duty to find a wife."

"My duty? I suppose you are thinking of my parents. Yes, but we don't feel as strongly about this as you Chinese do. Of course they would like me to marry and have children, but they are willing to let me do this in my own time."

"Don't you want to get married?"

Peter's reply to Wang Ming's question was delayed when a ball thrown by Bill bounced into his lap. Joshua, diminutive in size but a keen Christian, took this opportunity to say, "You have to wait for God to show you. You can't just marry anyone you like."

He paused for a moment. "Joshua is right. A Christian must wait for God to show him."

"You will be very lonely," Wang Ming observed, "if you don't find a wife."

"Why are you so anxious to see me married? Maybe I will be so busy looking after my children that I won't have time for you guys any more." The students sitting with him grinned.

Joshua stood up. "I must go and buy a new hymn book."

"Have you sung all the ones out of your old book?" Peter asked him. The strains of his hymn singing could often be heard in the hostel.

"There's a new one just published. It looks very good."

The others stood up too. It was time to rest. By taking a rest in the afternoon, they would have the strength to study past midnight. Peter found it hard to sleep in the daytime, but even he found it a good thing in the hot weather to lie down for half an hour. Crossing the courtyard, he was conscious that the wind was getting a bit stronger.

As he entered the Japanese building that he was learning to call home, he removed his shoes and shuffled into his slippers. . A short walk down the corridor brought him to the kitchen. From the refrigerator he took a small melon, which he sliced in two and took with him to the study. This room was large enough for meetings, which, up to now, had merely been informal English classes. Along one wall, on fitted shelves, were displayed a few Bible commentaries, devotional and doctrinal books, works of English literature for use in his teaching and a few novels. Most of his books he had left at home, as it would have been too expensive to bring them here. The opposite wall held sliding doors. There was just one plain wall surface, which held a clock and a university matriculation photograph.

On the desk, which stood in a corner, there were pictures of his family in Keswick and some Lakeland scenes.

Although he had been here less than two months, it was beginning to feel like home. After those two years of language study in Taipei, it was good to be back to a regular schedule.

He reflected again on the concern his students had shown for his marriage. He had not told them about Cynthia. There was so much uncertainty about that relationship that he preferred to keep quiet about it.

He looked at the thermometer. 92 degrees! It was probably about 90% humidity too. The bedroom was the place for him. He lay on the bed with the fan whirling above him and picked up the Thackeray novel that he was currently reading. After half an hour spent like this, he would have sufficient strength for his afternoon tasks.

4

The clock at the bookshop registered nearly half past one as Joshua pushed open the door and stepped inside. Arnold Maguire, balding slightly and in his mid forties, was just opening a box of new books. He gave a smile of welcome: Joshua was a regular customer, though his financial constraints as a student did not permit him any lavish expenditure.

Joshua sought to describe the hymn book that he wanted. "Yes", said Arnold in his best Mandarin, "I think we have one left. I did not realize they were going to be so popular. I must order some more. Is this the one you mean?"

"That's right," Joshua said. Is it 25 NT$?"

"Yes." The transaction was soon completed, but Joshua lingered to finger through other books, which he could not afford to buy.

Miss Lee came out from the back room, yawning and bleary eyed. How anyone could sleep on an upright chair in a small and stuffy room Arnold did not know; but it was an art which the locals had perfected.

"I'll be back in a couple of hours," he told her.

"No problem," she replied.

Arnold mounted his motor bike, which was parked just outside the shop. Although his home was quite near, he did not wish to waste time walking. He was getting into a rut. At one time the idea of doing missionary work had been vested in glamour; but spending a lot of time behind the counter in a bookshop somehow did not fall into this category. He could have done such a job as this without leaving his own country.

But it was not a good idea to daydream in such circumstances. A motorcyclist with a red peaked cap came zooming towards him on the wrong side of the road, just missing him by inches. A yellow-capped schoolboy on a pushbike that was much too big for him wobbled into his path and out again. He had to swerve to avoid a large pile of sand left in the roadway by some builders. Maybe it was a life of danger and excitement after all! He turned into Lane 147, turned again on to Alley 41, and drew to a halt in front of the gate of his home. The best thing about being a married missionary was that home was not somewhere thousands of miles away, but here in Taiwan, just a short distance from his place of work.

He let himself in with his key. Immediately Philip, his 4-year-old, came running up to him. "Daddy's come back!" he shouted. "A big hug, Daddy!" Daddy was happy to oblige.

"Where's Mummy?" he asked.

"Mummy's in the kitchen. Dinner's ready. I've eaten mine."

"You didn't want to wait for your Daddy?"

"Mummy said I could."

"And what about Sammy?" Sammy was his 2-year-old son.

"He went to sleep. He hasn't eaten yet."

It was great to be able to speak so freely with his older son. It seemed like only yesterday that the noises which his son made were hard to decipher; but now he spoke very clearly, and it was a joy to communicate with each other. Sometimes, however, it was difficult to get him to stop talking.

In the kitchen, Kathleen, a slight figure with long black hair, was ladling out the soup. They embraced, and Philip clutched his leg as a means of inclusion. Philip went off to play with his new building blocks and Arnold sat down to eat with his wife.

"Anything interesting happened?" she asked.

"The usual trickle of customers. Pastor Wang says he's moving to Taipei. Pastor Chou's wife is out of hospital. Oh, and we were discussing taking the book van out tomorrow to the Pingyuan area. Last time the people there showed a lot of interest." The use of a mobile bookshop was a new development, and it was much appreciated by rural folk. People would gather round simply out of curiosity, and this provided good opportunities to talk about the gospel. Normally he had the company of Robert Chang, a recent graduate who was considering full time Christian service.

"You know we'll miss you. But we know how much you value those trips."

As he sat down to eat, Arnold picked up the English newspaper from the table. Almost immediately he was laughing. This made Kathleen curious. "This is priceless," he stated. "There is a fellow here who was charged 12,000 NT$ for his electricity."

"I admit that prices have gone up a lot, but that does seem a bit steep."

"You haven't heard the whole of it, sure you haven't. They accidentally wired him up to the traffic lights. The council agreed to recompense him."

"And so they should. Now, how about having your soup before it gets cold?"

"Sorry. I don't know why we buy that 'paper. Sure, there's never much in it. But it's worth it for the odd funny story. Keeps me sane."

"And it's good to be able to read something in English."

After a pause he continued: "Sometimes, you know, I wonder if I did the right thing. I was doing a good job with the newspaper in Belfast. I could have gone a long way."

"But you could never have lived with yourself if you had stayed there when God wanted you to do something else."

"Sure, I'm not saying I regret anything. Just thinking aloud, that's all."

"And don't criticize the local rag by your perfect standards. I'm sure they are doing their best."

Soup and sandwiches were followed by melon. At this point, Philip returned, brandishing his toy sword. "I want banana, Mummy,"

"Here you are," Kathleen said, opening one for him. It was still green, but quite edible. "And next time, young man, accept all you are given during meal time."

Philip strolled off with his new acquisition, and his parents finished off the melon. After this they washed up together. The kitchen was not very big and most of the cupboards were either too high or too low. But it was still better equipped than many of the Chinese kitchens. Considering the disadvantages,

Kathleen was very good: she rarely complained.

It had not been easy for them to adjust to married life after being single missionaries for some time. It was harder for Kathleen than for himself. Formerly she had been involved in church work, which included pastoral visiting and Bible training in the London suburbs. She had come to Taiwan with dreams of great things; but now it was house and family that occupied most of her time, and she could easily feel under-used. From time to time he would reassure her that she was doing an important job. Although she accepted what he said, he could still trace some unease.

As for Arnold, he greatly enjoyed this domestic life. As a boy, however, he had had a great thirst for adventure. He had enjoyed reading stories of missionary heroes, who seemed adept at getting themselves into tough situations, but always came out on top. In his present life the most dangerous thing he did was contend with traffic. There were no menacing cannibals here, and if there were deadly snakes he had yet to encounter them. When he went on furlough and spoke about his work, it did not sound particularly exciting: people would not want to hear about maniacal taxi-drivers and ferocious motor cyclists.

The last dish was washed, wiped and replaced (on tip-toe) in the appropriate cupboard. Now it was time to lie down for a little while. Philip would play happily on his own, and they should be able to get a little rest.

Just as they were about to make for the bedroom, however, Sammy appeared at the door, clutching his blanket. "Dinner!"

he said. Here was someone who knew how to draw maximum effect from a minimum of vocabulary.

5

When she was free to do so, Rose liked to take an afternoon walk. As the sun was strong, she took with her a sunshade. In such a society, this was not unusual, for the palest of the Chinese girls were regarded as the most beautiful. For Rose it was not so much a question of beauty as of protection. Her northern skin did not take kindly to an overdose of sunshine, especially when temperatures were in the 90s.

You could never get bored walking along these streets. Here was a man with a mug in one hand and a toothbrush in the other, vigorously brushing his teeth and spitting into the gutter. A little further on, people were bringing their rice to a man with a portable machine that would turn it into something that could be used as a breakfast cereal if you were Western, but the local people made it into little cakes. Further on, a woman was setting bowls of fruit before a family shrine, and adding joss sticks to complete the offering.

She came to the level crossing. The barrier was down, and cars and motor bikes were stretched right across the road, waiting for a chance to move; when the barrier went up again it was like the Charge of the Light Brigade, except that nobody was injured. She turned to walk beside the railway line.

That morning she had received a letter from her sister Ethel. Another baby on the way! It was due around February. Rose was very happy for her, though she felt a little pang within her.

It had been hard to accept that a call to the mission field might also be a call to singleness. She felt she would have much to offer as a wife and mother, but maybe that was not to be. When word got round that Peter was coming to live in this area, there was a lot of speculation. They were both single, both of the same age, both British. A match made in heaven. That was what people inferred. This made her all the more determined to confound their expectations. She was not going to throw herself at the first man who came along – even if he should be the only one.

So far they had not had much chance for conversation, as their paths crossed little. There was already in existence a little meeting organized on Sunday evenings for prayer and fellowship. Maybe Peter would be a part of that. However she was still determined that, should this bring them together, she would not see it is a means to develop a deeper relationship.

A train clattered past. It was a 'putung che' – the very slow kind that halted at every possible stop. She had taken one once, but never again. It would almost have been quicker to walk! The good thing about the train system was that you had such a wide choice of trains, some quicker some slower, and a range of fares to go with it. You got what you could afford.

She could imagine Ethel bringing her son when he was a little older. He would be fascinated by these trains. It would be lovely if family members could come out some time. She would take great delight in showing them round. Maybe her parents would not make it, however, for they were getting on.

She preferred to walk later in the day when it was a little

cooler, but on this particular day she had an English class at that time. There was such a thirst for English. People saw it as a passport to success. She could have spent all her time doing this, but she tried not to let it dominate her time. She hoped they would not all pick up her Blackburn accent, though it was not as strong as it had once been. American accents were more common among local English speakers, even among people who had never been there.

From the railway, she turned sharp right so as to head back to the college. She was not really looking for romance, despite her loneliness. Surely God could help her to be content with her single life. He had helped her up till now. A pity she did not have more friends who would enjoy a bit of fun. Giving herself to the Lord's work meant that she was prepared for any limitations that this imposed. These walks were becoming more and more times for dialogue with the Lord. After all, prayer was not to be restricted to one little space of time in the early morning.

It would be good if you could look ahead to the immediate future. But it was also good not knowing. Life would be dull if everything was predictable. Already she could see the college in the distance. Just a short walk, but she had still worked up a sweat. It would be better when winter began, so as to bring some respite from this heat.

6

The hands of Alleyne Zimmer's watch pointed to five minutes

to three. This watch, plain but reliable, had been given to her four years earlier by a grateful student. She closed her copy of "Moody Monthly" and gathered up her books for her lecture. Sandy looked up from the chair where he was lying, cocked his ear and began to wag his tail.

"No, Sandy," said his mistress, "you know very well that it is not time for your walk. I'm going to class. You will get your walk at the usual time this evening."

As she came through the door into the open air, she almost tripped over the shoe repair man, who was sitting on the step, hammering a new sole into place. He gave her a nod of deference as she passed. A path diagonally bisected the college garden. This was her normal route to the lecture rooms. Some of the bushes, she noticed, were getting overgrown and needed a good pruning. Hsiao the gardener never seemed to notice these things for himself. She reached the classroom block and mounted the stairs.

The hubbub of conversation that came from Room 203 ceased abruptly as she entered. The members of the class stood to greet her and then collapsed back into their seats.

"Please turn to Isaiah 5," she instructed. The class obeyed. "There are many ways in which the relationship between God and his people may be described," she began. "Sometimes God is the Shepherd and his people the sheep. Sometimes God is the husband and his bride is the Church – which may be a difficult image for you males to contend with." (For a moment she thought of that decision she had made toward the end of that never to be forgotten furlough.) "Sometimes we see God as the husbandman and his people as the vine. That is the picture we are looking at this afternoon."

She looked up from her notes to study their faces. This was not one of her better classes. In fact, there were several students concerning whose progress she really despaired. One such student was Alice, on the back row, who seemed to spend more time with her eyes closed than open.

"Li-su, would you care to read the first four verses for us?" "Li-su" was Alice's Chinese name. She preferred to use their original names wherever possible. Alice looked up startled. After consulting with her neighbour, she stood up and began hesitantly to read.

It was toward the end of this reading that Miss Zimmer became aware that one member of the class was absent. "I don't see Ke-lin. Does anyone know where she is?" The silence that greeted her suggested that nobody did. "Fu-lang, you know her well. When did you last see her?"

"It was before lunch, when she came to see you," Florence replied.

"Well, she isn't here with us now. Where did she go?"

"I don't know. I didn't see her."

"I thought you were her best friend. Didn't you eat lunch together?"

"I didn't see her at lunch. She must have eaten somewhere

else."

"What about after lunch in the dormitory?"

"She didn't come back. She must have gone out somewhere."

"Then let us hope she remembers us and comes to class, even if she is late."

For the rest of the class, this was an excuse to let their minds wander. But not for long. "Then let us resume our study of Isaiah. This is a story about a vineyard. The owner of the vineyard did all he could to ensure a good yield."

7

Peter sat at the desk, completing his letter. A fan kept him cool, but the downside was that it kept trying to tug the aerogramme away from his grasp. He did not know why he kept writing to her. Maybe one day he would just stop.

It had begun when he was a curate in Manchester and Cynthia was a member of the choir. He was well aware that, as a single curate, he would be sought after, and he was usually very careful to avoid any unhelpful entanglements.

One day, at a choir practice, Cynthia was hobbling. She explained that she had fallen at work and damaged her knee. Because of this, he had offered to drive her home and she had accepted. She had invited him in for cocoa with her mother and herself, and he had agreed to it. After that she had eyes only for him, and he had to admit that he also warmed to her company.

It grew from this small beginning. His busy ministry did not leave him a lot of spare time; but they made space for walks and for visits to a coffee shop. In his position, it was impossible to keep such a relationship quiet, and he knew that the whole parish was aware that something was going on.

Neither of them had looked far into the future. It was a casual relationship, with very limited physical intimacy. They did not talk about marriage, though it was a possibility which they did not discount.

It all changed when he made a visit back to Keswick to see his parents and attended one of the Convention meetings. It was the missionary day, and the speaker that afternoon issued a bold challenge. He felt an overwhelming urge to offer himself for work overseas. After the meeting, he went to see a representative from one of the big missionary societies, who encouraged him to take things further. A trip to London brought that whole possibility much nearer.

On his return he confided this to Cynthia. Her reaction surprised him. Surely there were enough people to convert in England. Why go right across the world to people who spoke a different language? He was surprised at her negativity. It also showed him that she had nursed higher hopes of a permanent relationship than he had imagined.

There was another visit to London for further interviews. Finally there was the visit at which a selection committee would make their decision. Sitting in a chair, facing a table at which this group sat was a formidable experience. However, they must have liked what they had heard, for they accepted him.

When he told Cynthia the news, she tried to persuade him that his gifts lay elsewhere. She said that she loved him and wanted to be with him, but not in some nasty place at the ends of the earth. He suggested that they should stop seeing one another, but she burst into tears and asked for a hug.

When he went away for a term at a missionary training college, they exchanged letters. He was full of enthusiasm for the training he was receiving; but she would ask him to consider whether he was making a mistake.

A few months later, he was about to set off on the coach to London, ready to make his outgoing flight. She came up to Keswick the day before on a day trip. They took a walk to Friar's Crag, discussing their relationship.

"It looks as if it ends here," he exclaimed as they reached the end of the little peninsula. At the time he failed to appreciate the ambiguity of the remark.

"That sounds very final," she said.

"But if you don't share my vision for work in Taiwan, what's the point? It isn't as if we were ever deeply committed to each other."

"Don't say that," she said.

"Then would you come out with me?"

"I don't know. I would have to think about it. But I love you, I really do. I can't just say goodbye like that. We can write."

So that is what they did: they wrote. He described the sights and sounds of Taiwan, and she gave him the latest news from his old parish. He imagined the relationship would gradually fade into nothing, but up to now there was no sign of this happening. They each wrote once a week. It was a long time since either of them had even mentioned the possibility of being together in Taiwan. It was like travelling on a train that had no destination.

He had written the usual kind of letter. More news of the work in which he was involved. Some vague suggestions of affection. Nothing more. In a way, he wanted to end all this, but he did not have the heart to do it.

So here was his latest letter, ready for posting. He got to his feet, reached for his shirt, which was hanging on a nail, and slipped it over his shoulders. A short walk down the path to the front gate, and he was out on the street, heading for the post box, which was only a few yards away. It was only a short walk, but he was sweating profusely when he got back. Maybe if the wind got stronger it would cool things down.

8

Later that afternoon, Arnold was sitting in the little room behind the shop, the fan whirring rapidly as he discussed with

Robert Chang the next trip with the book van. Robert had graduated from the local university, done his statutory military service, and was now contemplating a permanent job. For the present, however, he was content to go with Arnold on these trips.

"We can leave at 8.30 tomorrow morning," Arnold suggested.

"How long does it take us to get to Pingyuan?"

"You should know. You're the local man. I reckon just over an hour. We should be able to set everything up by 10 o'clock. Pastor Yang at the Presbyterian Church will give us some lunch and a place to rest. Then in the afternoon we can go on to Lanying, which is about 40 minutes' drive. That should be a good visit. Last time a lot of people showed interest. You weren't with us that time, were you?"

"No, I had to go to see my grandmother. She was ill. Sorry I missed that."

"It was a good visit. There were a lot of people who showed interest. They asked a lot of questions. There was a Mr. Wei. He was very keen,. Maybe we will see him again this time."

When he talked about the book van, Arnold could not disguise his enthusiasm. The work in the shop was satisfying, but when he got out on the road he had a spirit of adventure. You never knew what you were getting yourself into. Sometimes it was just like being a pioneer evangelist. In a way, taking the books out was just an excuse. What really mattered was encounters with outsiders, many of whom had no connection with a church.

"Shall I check the van?" Robert asked.

"I would really appreciate that." It was good to have an assistant who had some gifts as a mechanic. The van had seen better days, and if it came to a stop Arnold would not know how to get it started again."

He heard Miss Lee's voice from the shop. "He's in the back room. Do you want to speak to him?"

Almost immediately, a figure came charging into the room. Robert politely excused himself. It was Pastor Fan, who ran a lively church in a northern suburb of the town. "Ah, Mr. Ma, he called. "Your assistant told me I would find you here."

This pastor was always somewhat overbearing. Some people felt that this man and his church were too threatening. It was all about healings, being filled with the Spirit, prophesying and so on. "You ordered those books for me?" he boomed.

"Yes, I did."

"Have they come?"

"Not yet. It was only the beginning of the week."

"A pity. I wanted to use them on Sunday."

"I'll let you know as soon as they come in."

"Please do. Oh, and take a look at this." He handed Arnold a flyer. Arnold tried to understand the Chinese.

"Evangelistic meetings. Next March . An American. You must have heard of him. In English he is called Paul Fennigan."

"I don't think so."

"Really? But he's really well known. We are lucky to have him. I hope you can advertise the meetings in the shop. God has greatly used this man. It is a big opportunity."

Arnold always found him overwhelming. This time was no exception.

"Must go. I have other things to do. Don't forget to tell me when the books come in." With these words he swept out of the room, leaving a draught which accorded well with his name.

Arnold was glad to relax after that brief encounter. Pastor Fan held strong views on the importance of evangelistic meetings, which in Chinese were called 'budauhui'(pronounced bu-dow-hwei). It was as if the churches could not function without someone coming from outside every so often and preaching to the masses. He wondered how much these churches understood about the more humble task of personal evangelism. Pastor Fan had persuaded the other ministers that such events were essential to the ongoing life of the churches, and who could speak against a man of such enthusiasm?

He looked at his watch. It was time to relieve Miss Lee at the counter, as she needed to go and prepare supper for her elderly mother.

9

Next morning, as she approached the gates of the college, Rose hoped she would not run into Miss Zimmer. It was absurd to feel like this. Any normal person would feel that getting one's hair done was perfectly justified. After all, most people liked to look their best. To Miss Zimmer, however, the proper stance for missionaries was to have your hair made into a bun. You were almost made to feel that she had the authority of Holy Writ for this, and that anyone who chose to make her hair look more attractive was akin to the whore of Babylon. At present, however, the wind had just spring up, and it threatened to undo all the good work.

"You look very beautiful," one of the male students said to her in his best English as she cycled past him. That was more like it. Why could not others be like that?

She continued on past the dining room and came to the block for single staff. As she turned the key in the lock, she felt a sense of relief. It was true that she would come face to face with Miss Zimmer sooner or later, but by that time her 'crime' would have lost its immediacy.

Rose decided to make herself a simple lunch and to cook a good meal in the evening. For anyone who thought of making herself another Fanny Craddock, the facilities discouraged such an ambition. Several of the commodities which were thought to be essential for good cooking in a Western environment were simply not available in the local shops. Her own equipment, a gas burner with two rings, also limited her choice. However, she was still able to produce food that had more nutritional value than the cook at college, with a limited budget, could produce.

Just as she was contemplating what to prepare, there was a knock on the door. She opened it to find Florence standing there.

"Am I disturbing you?"

"Not at all. Do come in."

"This won't take long," the girl assured her.

When they were seated, Rose asked, "Are you feeling better?"

"Oh yes, much better. It was nothing, really." She had not been so dismissive the previous day.

"I'm glad. You had us worried for a bit."

"Li Lausu, there is something I wanted to ask."

"Go ahead."

"I wondered – have you seen Catherine today?"

"No, I don't recall seeing her since the accident."

"She has disappeared. She did not go to class yesterday, and she did not come back to the dormitory. I am worried. This is not like her."

"There is probably some simple explanation."

"I hope so. She's my best friend, and if she was going somewhere she would tell me."

"Promise me that the moment you see her you will come here and let me know."

"Of course. And if you see her, please tell me." Rose was glad to see this sense of mutual concern among her students.

When Florence had gone, Rose thought more deeply about the matter. Catherine was always so predictable. Such behaviour was out of character. Had she gone off of her own accord, or was there a more complex explanation?

10

Alleyne Zimmer chose her friends carefully. She held back from becoming too intimate with her fellow-workers in the seminary. It seemed good to her to observe a working relationship but nothing more.

As for the other missionaries in the city, many of them were much younger than herself and did not seem very dedicated.

However, there was one woman who qualified. Helen Binch was about the same age as herself. She came from Edmonton, Alberta. Although she did not have the distinction of being born in China or even of having served there, and, indeed, had only entered upon missionary work in her middle years, she appreciated the same values as Alleyne did. She maintained traditional views, she observed Chinese customs without being too much swayed by her Western background and she believed that if a job was worth doing it was worth doing well.

Her job was to teach at a girls' school. Indeed, teaching had been her profession ever since she graduated from college. She was good at it, and commanded a lot of respect in the school and beyond it. Although the school had some limited accommodation to offer, she chose to live in a small apartment on the edge of the city, with no Western neighbours. When people expressed their concern about her living alone, she would brush off their criticisms by declaring that Taiwan was one of the safest places to live.

The two of them had met a few years earlier at a missionary retreat and soon became good friends. Every so often they would meet up. Both agreed that having such a friendship had given more meaning to their lives. On this day, they had agreed to go out for a lunch of dumplings in a quiet street behind the market.

Just as she was leaving the college, she came upon Rose. At first she hardly recognized her. What had she done to her hair? These flighty young missionaries were far too preoccupied with their own appearance. She would have been content with a mere nod in passing, but Rose seemed to want to talk with her.

"Have you seen anything of Catherine?"

"I assume you mean Ke-lin. No, I have not seen her today."

"I'm worried about her. She's missing."

"Missing? How can she be missing? I saw her yesterday."

"She wasn't in her dormitory last night."

"Then maybe she's gone home."

"She would not go off just like that without telling anyone."

"She told me her mother was in hospital."

"I didn't know that."

"And I said that if she was having trouble with the fees the committee might be able to help her."

"I'm sure she appreciated that. Was she in your class yesterday?"

She did not take kindly to this interrogation. "No, I didn't see her. But I didn't read anything sinister into that."

"I think we should try to find her. Did she have anything on her mind?"

"As I've told you, she was worried about her mother's health and her school fees."

"That doesn't sound like an excuse for running away," Rose admitted.

"Some people don't need much excuse. She will probably turn up soon."

"I'm rather worried about her. I must make some more enquiries."

"If you feel you should." It seemed unnecessary. There was probably a very good explanation. However, if Rose wanted to play Sherlock Holmes, who was she to stop her?

"I will let you know if I come up with anything. It's a bit awkward to get to Lanying by bus. Better to try the hospital. You don't happen to know which hospital?"

"No. She didn't tell me."

"What's the nearest hospital to Lanying?."

"That would be Yangli, I expect. I can't think of any other hospitals in that area."

"Thanks for that. I will try to follow that up."

"I wish you well with your investigations. In the meantime, I have an appointment to keep."

It was probably all a lot of bother about nothing. This would not be the first time one of the students had disappeared and reappeared again. They had their reasons. After this delay she would be a few minutes late for her lunch with Helen.

11

Peter's study was well equipped for dealing with hot weather, with its sliding panels and netting. By opening these panels, he could ensure that there was a flow of air to make living a little more comfortable. However, as he was sitting this Saturday morning at his desk finishing off the sermon, which he would be delivering at the English service the next day, he had the panels almost closed because of the increasing strength of the wind.

Local Episcopalian Christians were able to go for a Chinese service to Good Shepherd Church, where Rev. James Yang would cater for their needs. In this Japanese house, however, there was a small room which could be used as a church for English speakers. This was a new venture for Peter. On this coming Sunday they would meet for the first time. Publicity has been sent to the American military base, and it was possible that someone from there would join in the worship. The students also knew about it, and it was conceivable that a few of them might come either out of curiosity or in order to practise their English. Peter was looking forward to this experiment.

Suddenly there was a tap at the door. He looked round to see

Paul, one of his students, standing there with a girl. He invited them both in and poured them some juice.

"I wanted to introduce Jenny," Paul told him, blinking behind his spectacles. He spoke in English. "She belongs to my church." Paul was a Lutheran Christian, and was accustomed to worshipping at a church about a mile away. Jenny was an attractive girl, but, like many local girls, lacking in sophistication. Peter found this so refreshing after his experience of girls in the West. "I hope I'm not interrupting anything," Paul went on.

"Not really. I was just finishing my sermon for tomorrow. It is nearly done."

"That is good then. Jenny and I are good friends. I have told her a lot about you, and she said she would like to visit you."

"Pleased to meet you," Jenny said in her best English.

Peter felt very happy. It was obvious that there was deep feeling between the two young people. They seemed ideally suited to one another.

"Jenny's father is a pastor near Taichung. She is also studying at the university."

"What are you studying?" Peter asked.

Jenny was hesitant, as if she were trying to answer in English. Paul, with no such ambitions, explained in Mandarin, "She is studying chemistry. We are in the same department."

"So that is how you met?"

"And I now I have to take her back to the dormitory. I will be back for lunch."

Paul had a motor scooter. No doubt, Jenny would ride side saddle, as girls usually did in Taiwan. They always managed to look so demure and controlled, despite hazardous journeys among thronging traffic.

"Take care," Peter warned. "The wind's getting up and it is looking like rain."

When they had gone, he resumed the task at his desk. For a moment his thoughts turned to Cynthia. Would their relationship ever flourish, or would it remain uncertain? He found himself envying Paul his uncomplicated relationship.

12

Arnold had not listened to the weather forecast. After all, unbroken sunshine could normally be taken for granted. The clouds, the wind and the threat of rain had therefore come as a disappointment. He had discussed the matter with Robert, and they had decided they would still make the trip as arranged.

Because of the effect of this minor typhoon, the morning visit to Pingyuan with the van had been disappointing. Not a lot of people showed interest. Only five books had been sold, but that was better than nothing. However, the Yangs, their hosts, were in good form. Mrs. Yang had produced some tasty beef noodles and they had rested for half an hour. Perhaps their experience at Lanying would be more positive.

The Yangs and their two little pigtailed daughters waved them off, and they set off to follow dusty side roads to the next stop. Robert was a good companion. He had been converted while at university in Taipei, and he was still very enthusiastic about his faith As they journeyed he had several spiritual questions which Arnold sought to answer as well as he could.

When they came to Lanying they stopped in the main square, opened the sides of the van to reveal the book displays and waited for some response. Arnold was looking for Mr. Wei, who had shown a lot of interest on the previous visit, but there was no sign of him. A group of small boys came up to satisfy their curiosity, and Arnold and Robert passed on some free booklets, which appeared to delight them. It was after that that the rain came back

Arnold stared at the scene around him. Not far away were acres of rice fields, shimmering in the hot sun. A 'granny' dressed all in black and with bound feet – something you did not see a lot of these days – who had been sitting on the step of her home, retreated indoors. There was a small temple, where a woman with a joss stick was bowing in worship: maybe she was looking for some kind of favour, for this was normally a pragmatic exercise. Outside the temple was a statue of a lion, Chinese style, which looked nothing like the real thing. A girl with a basket full of dirty clothes had been going down to the river to do her laundry, but this change in the weather sent her scurrying back again.

He tried to imagine himself as the Far Eastern correspondent of a well known newspaper writing about these people and events for readers at home. Often he had sought to cast himself in this mould. Had he really made the right decision when he turned his back on the career of journalism, went to Bible School and came here to Taiwan?

The truth was that nobody would be very interested in this backwater. They wanted to hear about places where there was violence, conflict, revolution, disaster and the like. He could have made a living travelling from one trouble spot to another, reporting on such momentous events. It would have satisfied his longing for adventure.

A young man with an umbrella came walking up and made contact with Robert, who then produced a book for him to peruse. He nodded, asked about the price, and happily walked off with his prize. Robert was encouraged to have made a sale at all under these conditions.

Arnold picked up a few more free leaflets, this time aimed at adults, and approached people who were watching from a distance from the shelter of their homes. Most people accepted them, though one older woman, with arms folded, looked at him suspiciously and refused the offer. A young woman appeared briefly at one of the windows. She looked familiar. Where had he seen her? In the bookshop? At the seminary? Maybe it was just his imagination.

When the rain stopped for a while, two or three people decided to find out more. This encouraged others to follow their example. Soon they were rifling through the books and asking questions. Arnold and Robert were well satisfied: this was what they had come to do. It was a lot better than simply sitting in the shop and waiting for someone to come in.

When they had been there for about an hour, a renewed onset of rain and a strengthening of the wind drove away any other prospective customers and Arnold and his assistant decided it was time to pack up and make for home. It had been a worthwhile visit, despite the limitations, but how Arnold longed for something bigger. Why was it always the day of small things? This was far more satisfying than simply standing in the shop, but he still felt that he could be better employed.

13

Rose was glad to get off the bus at Yangli. It had been hot and stuffy, and she had had to stand most of the way. Although she had only been in this small town two or three times, she thought she could remember where the hospital was.

Yes, there it was. The building was old and not very big. There was no driveway: it simply opened out on to the street. She walked quickly because of the rain. As she entered through the main door, she was immediately aware that there was no air conditioning as there would have been in the larger hospitals in towns and cities. The walls were a faded green in colour and looked as if they had not been painted for several decades.

At the reception desk a woman temporarily abandoned her

knitting and looked at her as if her presence was an intrusion. Rose said she was looking for a Mrs. Ma from Lanying. It was good that she could remember the family surname; though sometimes wives retained their maiden name and that made the situation more complex.

"Do you have her full name?"

"No, I'm afraid not."

"We only have one Mrs. Ma. Ward 3." From the size of the hospital, Rose guessed that they probably only had three wards.

The ward contained rows of beds packed fairly close together. There were plenty of visitors there. The extra bedding and the various cooking implements suggested that many of them slept and ate there. Many of the patients were on drips. She hesitated, for she had no idea what Mrs. Ma looked like.

"Can I help you?" a young nurse asked. She used English, on the assumption that Rose did not speak Chinese, but Rose replied in Taiwanese, which both surprised and pleased her.

"Yes, do you have a Mrs. Ma on this ward?"

"In the corner over there."

Rose observed a bed where the patient leaning back, her eyes grimacing with pain. Sitting with her were three young women, probably her daughters. As she walked up to the bed, she saw expressions of surprise on their faces.

"Is this Mrs. Ma?" Rose asked.

Two of them nodded and the other said. "Yes, it's our mother."

"And Ke-lin is your sister?"

"That's right," said the one with the voice. "You know her?"

"I'm from the college. I look after the girls in the dormitories. I heard that your mother was sick and I came here to see how she was."

The mother looked as if she was going to try to talk, but the daughter who was doing all the speaking told her to conserve her energy. "Our mother is not well. She has a lot of pain and they are trying to find out what is wrong."

"I'm sorry to hear that." Rose wanted to say that she was praying for her, but that was something they might not understand. Catherine had told her that the other members of her family were not Christians.

"I thought that Ke-lin might be here with you," Rose suggested.

"No, she stayed at the house to cook some supper for our Dad. He will be very hungry when he comes in from the fields."

"I understand. I'm sure he will be glad of her help."

"It is a good thing the school has a holiday at this time."

"Is that what she said?"

"Yes. She forgot to tell us beforehand and we were all surprised to see her."

"Did she say how long the holiday was for?"

"I think she said it was just for a few days."

Rose considered telling them there was no holiday, but thought better of it. The other two sisters did not take much interest in the conversation. They were too busy trying to comfort their mother, who was still wincing from the pain and uttering the occasional groan.

"Mother normally sells fruit at the market," the talkative sister explained, "but now she is too sick to do it."

It occurred to Rose that one of the others might have taken it on for a while, but it was not for her to make such suggestions. Maybe they had other work to do. Or maybe there was another sister to do that.

At this point Rose tried to exchange a few words with the mother, but she did not show any indication that she understood her. There were some people, especially in the villages, who could not conceive that foreigners would ever be able to speak Taiwanese. Maybe Mrs. Ma was one of them; or maybe it was simply the illness that distracted her.

The rest of the visit was not very productive. Communication with the patient was virtually nil, no further explanations were forthcoming, and even the talkative sister began to clam up. After a little while Rose politely excused herself.

As Rose walked back to the bus stop, although glad that she now knew what had happened to Catherine, she wondered why she had left so suddenly and pretended that there was a holiday. It was not convenient to go to Lanying, but she hoped Catherine would return to college soon and that they could talk together about the whole affair. Miss Zimmer had said that she had sought to encourage the girl, but was there more to it than that?

14

Alleyne Zimmer had a lot to think about as she walked home through the driving rain. It was a blessing to have a friend like Helen. She had always regarded herself as very self-sufficient. When she first offered for the mission field, it was a commitment that could well deny her the opportunity of any deep companionship. There had been a possibility at one stage of entering into marriage, but it had not seemed right, and she had turned it down. Living a single life was the result of her determination to serve God fully, and she was determined that there should be no regrets.

It was only recently that the thought had come to her that she had no real friends. It was true that many people respected her for her teaching and for her dedication, and she had received gifts and testimonials to that effect. She liked to think that she had influenced so many lives for good. In the college and even beyond she had many acquaintances; but it was hard to think of anyone who might be called a close friend.

Until recently their acquaintance had been very casual: it was only recently, after meeting at the bookshop, that their friendship had developed into something more. When they began to talk, they realized quickly that they had an affinity with one another. They visited each other's homes, even though Helen lived out in the sticks, and a close bond had arisen between them. Now they contrived to see each other at least once a week.

This development had surprised her. Her isolation had not bothered her until now. Perhaps it was growing older that had convinced her that she needed another person with whom she could share her deeper thoughts. She could not have developed such a relationship with anyone in the college, for there she wanted to maintain a professional difference; but Helen had the advantage of coming in from the outside.

It had been a pleasant lunch. The restaurant was plain enough, but the food was wholesome, and it gave them opportunity to share their thinking. After the meal they wandered round the shops together, choosing the ones that offered most respite from the rain. Now it was time to get back to her flat to do a bit of marking.

Just as she was coming in through the gate, she saw Rose again. The girl was positively ubiquitous. Not only that, but she seemed to have something to say.

Without any preamble, she said, "I know where Catherine, that is, Ke-lin is."

"So your detective work paid off. How was she?"

"I didn't actually see her. I went to visit her mother in hospital and talked with her sisters."

"And?"

"And she's back in her home village. Seems to be spending a long weekend there. They think the school is on holiday. That's what she must have told them."

"Is she coming back?"

"I think so. I wonder what prompted her to leave in the first place."

"Our last encounter was very positive. As I said, I told her that, if her mother was ill, the college might be able to offer her some help."

"And how did she react?"

"She seemed grateful. It was most odd that she should run away. But it was probably concern for her mother that made her leave."

"Yes, that seems to be the most likely explanation."

They parted company. As she opened the door of her flat to receive a welcome from Sandy, Miss Zimmer reflected on that last conversation with Ke-lin. Had she been a bit harsh in her criticism of her work? But surely any harshness had been offset when she talked about the mother's illness. All the same, it was a little worrying. What did her students really think of her? Did they appreciate her, or were they simply being polite at times?

15

The next morning towards 11 o'clock Peter was waiting for people to come to the worship service. There had been no English service at St. John's for two years as there had been nobody to take it, so this was, in fact, a new beginning. He had advertised the event at the American military base, amongst the seminary staff and amongst the students in the hostel, but he still did not know whether anyone would come.

This was so different from taking a service in a large church in Manchester, or even in his native Keswick. Here they would use a room in the house, suitably equipped with a large curtain for backdrop and with a cross hanging in its centre, together with a reading desk, a lectern and a table which could be moved aside if the room should be used for anything else.

He had prepared a message based on Hebrews 10 about 'the confidence of faith'; but he wondered whether it would be too heavy. The problem was that he did not know who would be in his congregation, so it was bound to be somewhat hit and miss.

There were so many new things to absorb – his teaching of English Literature at the university, his care for the students in the hostel and now this English-speaking congregation. It was for him a very satisfying life, and he was so grateful that he had obeyed the call to come to this distant place and begin a completely new chapter. With the hurdle of initial language study behind him, now he was free to enter without hindrance into any ministry that came his way. There was something in him that rejoiced in diversity.

Suddenly he was aware of visitors. It was an American family – husband, wife, son of about 12 and daughter of about 6.

"Hi," the man called out. "We're Tom and Vickie Eastwicker and this is Craig and Amy". There were smiles and handshakes. "We're from Seattle, just been here a couple of months." Peter showed them into the church, which they decided was 'kinda cute'.

Next to arrive was a young couple also from the army base. The man was much taller than the woman. "We're Rick and Marlene Bakker", the man explained. "We're from Conneticut and we just got married." Peter welcomed them and showed them into the church, where they immediately fell into conversation with the Eastwickers.

It was no surprise to Peter when Professor Bill Smythe and his wife Jennifer, Canadians from the seminary, turned up, for they were Episcopalians and he taught Church History there. Bill had a goatee beard which gave him a very distinct appearance. They introduced themselves to the service personnel and all seemed to be in good spirits.

Peter wondered whether any of the students would show up. Just as the service was due to start, three of them appeared. Colin's appearance was no surprise, as he had an Episcopalian background. Mark was there probably to practise his English, and the other student, to his surprise, was David, who preferred his Chinese name of Dai Ming. Already Peter was aware that he was worried about the standard of his schoolwork, and it was doubtful whether he would understand much of the service.

It seemed odd to get into his robes for a service in such a simple and informal setting, but he knew that this was expected of him. Despite the ceiling fan, it was hot inside these clothes, which were not made for subtropical climates.

As the service began, he surveyed the little congregation. How could you even try to speak in a way that was meaningful to a congregation that included a theological professor, a six year old girl and a Chinese student with very little English?

The service which they used had been put together for the needs of American Episcopalians, since the diocese had had a lot of links with the States, so the service personnel ought to be familiar with it. When he announced the first hymn and prepared to play the accompaniment on the little organ, Jennifer asked if he would like her to play. This was a pleasant surprise, and he readily agreed to this. The singing was poor.

So the service continued. When it was time to preach, he tried to be both simple and profound at the same time, which was virtually impossible. Half way through there was a long sigh from Craig, which did not inspire confidence.

At the end, he waited for their reactions. The three students slid away before he could ask them if they had understood.

Bill Smythe said, "Very thoughtful", which could have meant anything. The Bakkers thanked him politely and said they would come again.

Tom, however, was in no hurry to leave with his family. "That was good, real good," he said, pumping Peter's hand vigorously. "You must come round for a meal, some time, mustn't he, Vickie?" He turned his head for her approval. "There is no Mrs. er - ?"

"No. I'm still single."

"All the more reason, then, for you to come to us. And we have a branch of the Toastmasters here. You seem to be good at speaking, so I guess you would enjoy it. If you want to go I'll pick you up some time. Last Thursday evening of the month."

"That sounds interesting." What a lame reply he had given.

" Well, time to get back for something to eat. Be with you next week, of course. Take care."

The children looked relieved to be moving at last. Left to himself, Peter concluded that the opening service had gone quite well after all.

16

Sammy objected strongly to his removal from the bath. While Kathleen tried to get him into his pyjamas, he expressed his dissatisfaction by howling incessantly. When Arnold tried to remove Philip from the water he asked, "Two more minutes". Eventually he was persuaded to come out, though with great reluctance. Then, before they could stop him, he was running naked and wet through the house; and Sammy, wearing only his pyjama top, scrambled down from the bed to join in the fun. It was only after some decisive action that order was restored.

"Why is it," Kathleen asked, "that this happens on a Sunday when we are getting ready for the missionary fellowship meeting? I never feel I'm in a state of grace."

"You've still got half an hour to get back to normal," Arnold informed her.

"Half an hour. I remember when we were in language school in Taipei - that must have been just before we met – and we had a prayer meeting on Wednesdays. We all used to have a time of quiet preparation so that we would be in a spiritual frame of mind when the meeting started. That's all gone by the board."

"No regrets?" Arnold asked, raising an eyebrow.

"Of course not. I could never go back to the old life." They exchanged a brief kiss.

"I'm sure the Lord understands all about it," Arnold went on. "After all, he was the one who gave us these children. It's just a phase. Things will get easier later."

"I wonder," Kathleen said doubtfully.

When the children were encased in their pyjamas, it was time
for prayers. Sammy had to be brought out from under his bed,
and Philip had to be persuaded that wearing a toy rifle over his
arm (an unfortunate gift from a well meaning friend) was not
compatible with being a good soldier of the Lord Jesus Christ.

The boys were normally invited to suggest people for whom
they would like to pray, but this time they were in a sullen
mood and there was no response. Arnold uttered a few prayers
to which they gave a muted response. The devotions were now
completed and it was time for a story. Arnold selected a short
one and sat in a chair between the beds to read. "Once there
was a cat who lived in the-"

"Tree!" exclaimed Sammy, with a pointing finger.

"What's he doing?" asked Philip.

"I'm just coming to that. He lived in the country. All day long
he would run in the fields."

"Flowers," Sammy declared, pointing again.

"Yes, there are flowers."

"Who made the flowers?" Philip asked. "Did God make
them?"

"Yes, God made them."

"Why?"

"He probably wanted the world to look nice."

"Did he make the mud as well?"

"Yes, he made everything."

"Mud doesn't look nice."

"I'm sure he had a reason for it." You had to be a theologian if you wanted to answer the questions that children raised. Obviously it was not going to be a short story-time tonight. Eventually, after about twenty more questions, the adventures of the cat were brought to a successful conclusion, and, bidding the boys to go straight to sleep, Arnold left the room.

Even as he came out, the doorbell rang. It was Tim Holleron, who never left anybody in doubt of his Texas origin. "I guess I'm a little early," he grinned with a glance at his watch.

"That's all right," Arnold replied. It's nearly time."

"Who's that?" came a voice from the bedroom.

"Only Uncle Tim."

"Can I see him?"

"No, you're supposed to be asleep."

"I brought some doughnuts," Tim declared, handing over a white paper bag of them. " Five years yesterday since I first came to Taiwan. Sorta wanted to celebrate."

"Thanks," Arnold said. "I think Kathleen's just changing. She'll be with us in a moment." They both took a seat. "How's the teaching going?"

"So-so. Response is kinda slow. They think more of basketball than anything else."

"But that's normal for boys, isn't it?"

"Yeah, I guess so, but I wish there was a bit more to show for it". He put a hand in his pocket to pull out his handkerchief, and inadvertently pulled out a wad of tracts.

The squeal of bicycle brakes announced the arrival of Sister Cecilia, the second visitor. Whatever the temperature, she always appeared immaculate in her grey habit. A dumpy figure, originally from Djakarta, she nevertheless had a good command of English. The first words she uttered as she stood at the door blinking were "Am I late?"

"Not at all, " Arnold assured her. "Do come in. We're still waiting for Rose and Big Lil. Peter is coming for the first time, and Kathleen is still changing."

"I liked her ok as she was," Tim quipped.

Cecilia sat in the hard wooden chair that she always favoured. Maybe the soft easy chairs would have been regarded as an unacceptable indulgence.

Kathleen came in with cool drinks and biscuits; and the doughnuts were added to the display. Sister Cecilia happily took the doughnut that was offered to her. Apparently this caused no qualms of conscience.

The bell sounded again.

"I'll get it," Kathleen offered.

17

One thing which Rose enjoyed about these Sunday evenings at the Maguires' was that she was inside a proper home. The small room assigned to her at the college did not feel like a home, and her relationship with the girls in the dormitory did not correspond to a normal home life, even though she cared deeply about their problems.

How she appreciated the fellowship of this little group of friends! Here she could communicate with others more openly than she could at the college. Often she felt that the fellowship she enjoyed here gave her strength to cope with the many problems that came up in her life and work.

She greeted the others and took her place on the red-cushioned chair by the door which was her normal place. Kathleen thrust a glass of Koolade into her hands and offered her a doughnut, which she rightly assumed had come from Tim. A call came from the boys' room for a drink of water, and Kathleen went out to answer it.

The bell rang again. This time it was Big Lil. So named because of her size, she was a Canadian Pentecostal, who had opened her own little church in the city. She had a reputation for driving out demons, and it was thought that they ran for their lives when they saw her approach. "And how are you all, my dears?" she beamed.

"That's everybody except Peter," Arnold announced. "He said he would come for the first time tonight." At that moment the bell rang.

Rose had seen him briefly on a few occasions, but they had never sustained a conversation. He apologized for being late, as he had had trouble finding the house. Arnold introduced him to the rest of the group, and when Kathleen returned she took her place at the little harmonium ready for the start of the meeting.

They began with a song called 'Alleluia', which they all knew well. Sister Cecilia requested the hymn 'Lead, kindly light'. (This 'kindly light' had led Newman into that very fold to which she now belonged.) They sang two more hymns, after which Arnold suggested a time of praise and prayer. Although they followed no set liturgy, it was usually predictable the way things would go. The meeting was normally vaguely charismatic, so there was also a place for the unexpected.

Rose joined heartily in the expressions of praise. It was usually Tim who slipped from praise into intercession and the others followed suit. Soon they were praying for various missionary friends who did not belong to the group. Arnold was praying for Miss Zimmer. It was strange that a woman with such high ideals did not attend this fellowship meeting. It was as if she was afraid of forming close relationships. Sometimes too she would be critical of missionaries who spent too much time together when, in her opinion, they ought to be out amongst the Chinese serving and witnessing. She was also known to be critical of anything charismatic. Rose realized that she was letting her mind drift, and she forced herself to listen to the next prayer that was being made.

A silence ensued. Arnold asked whether anyone would like to contribute some teaching or some testimony. Sister Cecilia told how the Lord had enabled her to give a gracious answer when one of the other sisters was unkind to her. Kathleen told how God had answered her prayer when Philip got tonsillitis. Tim said there was a verse in Deuteronomy that he had found very helpful, but when he tried to look it up he could not find it. Big Lil described a long struggle for the soul of a blind woman who, in the end, was gloriously saved.

After a while, Arnold invited the group to mention specific requests for prayer. Rose asked: "There is a girl in the college whose mother is ill. She has left the college without permission for a few days. Can we pray that her mother will get well and that she will come back? I think she may have other problems too." Several of them prayed for this situation.

They went on to pray for Tim's earache and for Big Lil's awkward relationship with a co-worker. All in all, it was very much the usual content, but it was so helpful to pray and be prayed for in this way.

At the close there was a buzz of conversation. Nobody was eager to leave. People welcomed Peter and expressed the hope that he would feel free to join in more on his next visit.

Her red bicycle was still leaning against the wall of the house, suitably locked, of course. Rose and Peter found that they would be cycling home in the same direction, so they cycled together.

"I hope you didn't find it too strange," she said.

"Not at all. I used to go to a meeting in Taipei that was very similar."

"That'll be at the Dukes'? Yes, I've been there too. We're a strange assortment, but we get along together."

"I can see that." He swerved to avoid a mangy dog that had crossed his path. On a narrow alley like this there was not a lot of room.

"You take your life into your hands every time you get on a bicycle here," she commented, "but we survive."

"You live in the seminary then?"

"Yes, it's a bit cramped, but I manage. How do you find the hostel?"

"A bit different from your place. I have lots of room. I could bring up a whole family there and still have space."

"I wish I had more space."

They came to a place where their ways separated. She reflected that Peter was friendly and easy to get on with, but she had no plans to take their relationship any further. Within this group, there was safety in numbers.

18

Alleyne Zimmer laid down her pen. She had been writing to a prayer partner in Atlanta. This was a duty which she always took very seriously. In fact, she could not think of a single letter to which she had not replied. If people took the trouble to write to her, it was important that she should write back.

Now it was time for her pre-bedtime ritual. She would normally spend ten minutes walking the dog, ten minutes drinking a cup of tea and reading a devotional book and then a few minutes cleaning her teeth and changing into her night attire.

Sandy always knew when his walk was due. Already he was lying near the door with his tail thumping vigorously. "Ready for your walk, Sandy?" she asked. The question was quite unnecessary, but it was part of the ritual. She fastened the collar round his neck and the adventure was able to begin.

It was only by pulling hard on the leash that she was able to avoid being catapulted down the steps. Fortunately it had gradually been getting drier during the day. Once they were out in the open air, she noticed Rose wheeling her bicycle in through the gate. She must have been to that missionary fellowship meeting. It was not for her. How could you enjoy fellowship with people of such different backgrounds? There were even people from the Church of Rome. No, she preferred to mix with those whose Evangelical background was above dispute.

Her thoughts turned again to Ke-lin's disappearance. It was good to know that she was safe. But what had prompted her to go in the first place? If it was simply because of her mother's illness, the correct procedure would have been to inform the college authorities that she was needed at home. Was it anything she had said? Had she not gone out of her way to assure the girl that the college would give her any help that she needed? Suddenly she recalled how that conversation had started. Maybe she had been a bit too severe in her criticism of the essay. But surely a thing like that would not have made her run off in such a way! She knew that she could be a bit strict at times, but that was her personality. She had always believed in telling it straight. Why should it be any different on this occasion?

How familiar was the scene around her! They passed a place where young people were sitting with their late-night snacks. Although she was very much used to local customs and tried to identify as much as possible, this was something she did not do. At that time of the evening she preferred to be alone.

Another four years and all this would be behind her. That was hard to imagine. The life of this teeming Taiwanese city, with its long history, was very much her real environment, and the country of her nationality seemed remote and unfamiliar. The thought of retirement appalled her. Maybe they would find some way to let her stay on. Or, if not, maybe she could make her home here, even if the main work should be taken away from her.

So many young people these days came out to Taiwan as missionaries for a few years and then returned to their own country to live almost as if this had never happened. There was a time when a lifetime commitment was expected, and that was what she had been happy to give. For her, it was almost as if she had been born Chinese.

Soon the walk was over and it was time for that last cup of tea. She sighed happily. This was home. This was where she belonged. At that time she was not aware of the disruption that was to come.

19

On Monday morning Peter taught a class at the university. As usual, he cycled there, a journey of about ten minutes. He was faced with a sea of faces, some 60 or so in all, all ready to receive the jewels of wisdom that would issue from his mouth – or, at least, that seemed to be how they regarded it. Although some teachers in England would be glad to have such rapt attention, it annoyed him that there was such an exaggerated respect for the teacher and so little willingness to think for themselves.

This morning he wanted to introduce them to Wordsworth, and, in particular, to teach them to appreciate the poem 'Daffodils'. Whether daffodils were to be found in the Taiwan climate he was not sure, so he had brought a picture with him just in case it was needed.

At the end of this hour, he had to teach another class about Jane

Austen, but before he could get away one of the students came up to him. He seemed to be upset. "May I come and see you?" he asked.

"Of course; but I am just about to take another class."

"I will come to your house. When will you be there?"

"About 3 o'clock this afternoon. Do you know where to come?"

"Yes, I know. I'll be there."

The other class was just the same. The world of Jane Austen must have been just as obscure to them as the world of Wordsworth (it was the same period anyway), but there was still an eagerness to learn.

That afternoon he was sitting in his study when the student appeared. He immediately produced cold water for them both, and they sat in rattan chairs to talk.

"I'm sorry, I don't know your name. There are so many students in the class."

"Just call me Simon."

"Very well, Simon. Now why did you want to see me?"

"It's a family problem."

"Do you want to tell me about it?"

"It's about my father. We live in a small village not so far from here. People there follow the old customs. . I have always respected both my parents. My father follows traditional religions. But he has been in trouble."

"What kind of trouble?"

"He was accused by a neighbour of taking some money. Now my father would never do anything like that. He is a very honest man and he has brought me up the same way. But nobody believed him. And they put my father in prison."

"I'm really sorry to hear it. Is he there now?"

"Oh no. It was only for a few days. But it has made him very sad. He feels that he no longer has any honour in our village community. And I feel sad for him." He sighed, and cast down his eyes. It did not seem appropriate to say anything for a while. Then he lifted up his eyes again and said, "I had nobody to talk to. You seemed a kind man. That is why I wanted to talk with you."

"You can talk with me any time you like."

"Thank you. It helps me to talk. You are also a Christian?"

"Yes. It is because of my faith that I came here to Taiwan."

"I thought so. I wish I had your faith."

"You can have, if you want."

"I need to think about it. I wish I lived here in the hostel, then I would be able to talk with you more often. Do you have room for me?"

"All the places are filled; but one student is finding the work difficult and may be moving out soon. If he does, I will let you know."

"Sorry to hear about that, but if he has to leave that would be wonderful. I would like to live here."

After Simon had gone, Peter reflected on the incident. Here was a young man with a real sense of need, and if room could be found for him it might have a profound effect on him.

20

It was stocktaking time. This was not an activity which Arnold enjoyed, but he regarded it as a necessary evil. He remembered one Christian bookshop in Belfast where chaos prevailed, and where the manager was the only member of staff who knew where to find anything. He was determined that his own shop would never get like that. In any case, the proprietors of the chain for which he worked would never permit such slackness, or he would be looking for a new job.

It would have been easier if they could have closed the shop for the duration. Instead of that, Robert, Miss Lee or himself had to look available each time a customer came in. This slowed down the work, but it was preferable to trying to do the job out of shop hours, which would have taken him away from his family. The two assistant staff members got a bit irritable because of the extra demands of the job and he was glad it was only once a year.

He was like a child out of school when the day's work ended and they could, temporarily at least, leave this work behind them. Once again he climbed on his motorbike to make the short journey home.

Sammy and Philip were engaged in a dispute when he arrived, but when they saw him they came running to him for a hug.

"They've been like that all day," Kathleen complained. "I was getting to the end of my tether."

He gave her a kiss for consolation. Her face, lined with irritation, softened a little.

"Oh, and there's a letter for you," she went on.

When he opened it, he found that it was from Dick, a friend who had worked with him at the 'Belfast Telegraph'. In those days the two of them had simply covered social events, whilst hoping for some more challenging work After Arnold had left and gone into missionary work, Dick had risen to a much more responsible position. If he had remained, Arnold could have done the same. This letter, however, spoke of better things. Dick had applied for a job with the 'Times' in London, and had been accepted. Soon he and his family would be moving there to take on this challenge. They were currently looking for suitable accommodation, which could be pricey..

Arnold had to fight back the envy which came into his mind. He could well imagine himself in such a position. He had the skill for it; but God had led him into this new life, and it was not for him to complain.

Dick said that his old job at the 'Belfast Telegraph' would be vacant if Arnold felt like coming home. He smiled ruefully. It was overoptimistic to think that the newspaper would employ him in such a capacity when he had been out of the country and the profession for so long. No, he had burnt his bridges and must live with the consequences.

"Anything interesting?" Kathleen asked him.

"Dick has got a job at the 'Times'."

"In London? Good for him." She studied him for a moment. "You would have liked that job for yourself," she hinted.

"Yes, I would."

"You made a better choice." She squeezed his hand. This had become a frequent form of communication, in which words were unnecessary.

21

Rose felt a little cooler and fresher that evening after taking a shower. She was just putting on some earrings that she had recently bought when there was a tap at the door. To her surprise she found Catherine standing there.

"You're back!" she exclaimed.

"Yes. May I come in for a moment?"

"Of course"

They both sat down, and Catherine volunteered, "I just came to explain." She seemed a little nervous.

"I'm glad you did." Rose hoped she sounded reassuring.

"It was kind of you to visit my mother. I really appreciate that."

"It was good to meet her and your sisters. How is she now?"

There were tears in Catherine's eyes. "I think she is a little better, but she is still in hospital"

"If they can control the pain that will be something. Was it mainly because of your mother that you left so suddenly?"

"Partly. But there was something else."

"Do you want to tell me?"

"It was Sz Lausu. She made me afraid."

"Do you want to tell me about it?"

"I wrote an essay, but I could not write it very well because I was thinking of my mother. When I went to see her she scolded me. She said it was a very bad essay."

"And was it so very bad?"

"Yes, I think it was. But she did not have to be so angry. She really scared me."

"And how do you feel now?"

"Better. I don't think I'm afraid any more."

"Good. You have to make allowances for Sz Lausu. She has very high standards, and she can be critical of others when they don't reach such standards. I don't think she meant to frighten you. I think she just wanted you to give of your best."

"I try to. When my mother is getting better, I think I shall be able to do better work."

"Good. Now I had better let you go. You have some catching up to do."

Catherine looked very grateful. Now Rose faced the task of letting Miss Zimmer know that Catherine was back. What should she say about the reason for her absence? Probably it would not be wise to give the real reason. And yet, if she avoided this issue, the same thing could happen again. She sighed. Why did life have to be so complicated? Relating to Miss Zimmer and her standards was never an easy matter.

22

When the summons came to visit the Principal, Dr. Timothy Lee, Miss Zimmer had no idea what it was all about.

She was to meet him not in his office but in his home. It was his wife, Angela, a tall Scotswoman, who opened the door to her. She was all sweetness and light and showed her into a room which looked, in its furnishings, more Western than Chinese. Offered coffee, she asked for Chinese tea instead, and her request was granted.

Dr. Lee had only been there for four years. Most of his studies had been done in the USA. He was in his late thirties, which meant that he was only just into his teens when Alleyne was beginning her work at the seminary. No indication was given as to why she was being summoned. Surely it had nothing to do with that girl who had just come back from her unexpected leave. That was just a trivial matter.

He came into the room and sat in a chair opposite her. "You are quite a veteran, Miss Zimmer," he began, cupping his hands together.

"I like to think that my experience counts for something here."

"Of course, we value that."

"I have seen quite a few people come and go. But my motto has always been that if you are called to a job you stick at it unless you have a very clear call to go elsewhere."

"Very commendable, I'm sure."

She could tell by his fidgety movements that he was unhappy about something. The trouble with the Chinese was that they never got round to the point straight away. It could be quite a while before he came round to the reason for summoning her; so she decided to take the matter into her own hands. "Was there any special reason why you wanted to see me?"

"Well, I wanted to see if you are happy here, working with us."

"Perfectly happy. I think we have a good working relationship. There are, of course, one or two innovations which it has not been easy for me to adapt to, but overall I am satisfied."

Dr. Lee chose not to ask her what those innovations were. That was just as well, as it could have been rather embarrassing for both of them.

"As the principal, I'm responsible for the smooth working of this college. I've been making an exhaustive survey of our current situation."

"And did you come to any conclusions?"

"Yes. Not clear ones at this stage. But there are one or two adjustments which will have to be made in due course."

"What kind of adjustments?"

"Miss Zimmer, I gather you would have four more years of service to give before retirement?"

"Yes, I would like to go on longer than that, but I am not sure that my mission would be prepared to extend my contract. They are so much affected by their written policies. I would be perfectly happy to continue, and would bring pressure to bear on them, but I fear they will stick to their rules."

"So you do not feel happy about the prospect of retirement?"

"Mr. Principal, we are talking about something that is four years away."

Dr. Lee looked at his fingernails for a few moments, as if trying to determine what to say next. When he looked up again, he began, "We are looking at our staff needs, and the general feeling is that currently we are overstaffed. It would seem to be wise for us to cut down on numbers."

So that was what it was all about. He was trying to get rid of her. The shock went through her whole system. "Yes," she found herself admitting, "there are a few who are not pulling their weight – especially the younger ones. Maybe you would like me to suggest someone who could be asked to move on."

Dr. Lee looked more embarrassed than ever. "That was not quite what I was looking for, Miss Zimmer. You have only four years to go, and I think you are due for some leave next year."

"If I choose to take it."

"What would you think if it was suggested you retire early?"

At first she did not know how to reply. Then she said, "Dr. Lee, I am a woman of much experience. In a college where so many of the staff are young and inexperienced, I consider that my contribution is a valuable one. Are you suggesting that this experience counts for nothing? There is also the question of what my mission would make of such a suggestion."

"I am not suggesting anything. I am merely looking at remote possibilities. I'm offering you the choice of retiring early if you should prefer it. Now I'm not talking about today or tomorrow, or even next week. But, well, maybe next year...."

"Dr. Lee, I'm not in the habit of abandoning ship in the middle of a voyage. My supporters have been informed that I shall be here for four more years and they would be disappointed if they heard that I was going to leave before that time was over."

"As I said, nothing is to be decided right now. I'm merely looking at possibilities."

"Then that is one you can rule out. Dr. Lee, I have other things to do, and if you will excuse me ---"

"Of course. I know I have taken up enough of your valuable time."

She was glad to get out of the house and back into her own company. How could it even be thought that the college would be a better place without her? She felt deeply wounded. If any attempt should be made to dislodge her, she would resist it with every ounce of her being. That was the trouble when they appointed somebody so young as this principal!

23

That evening, Peter had just finished eating with the students. Limited to a small budget, old Su, the cook, did a good job. Although Peter was not eating big meals, and might even have lost a bit of weight, he found these meals were adequate for his needs.

On this occasion, Dai Ming was in an anxious frame of mind. He described how difficult his course was, and expressed concern lest he should have to give up. Peter had sought to encourage him, but there was not much he could do.

Now he was back in his own quarters, in the living room rather than the study this time, taking a welcome cup of coffee and eating a cookie from the Sunshine Bakery across the road. The proprietor had accumulated some American recipes, and his cookies were appreciated by a large clientele. Suddenly he thought he heard a tap on the outside door. On investigation he found that it was James Yang, the minister from Good Shepherd Church. "Fu Mushr" (He addressed him by his Chinese name.) : "Do you have time?"

"Yes, come in" He led him into the interior and offered coffee, but his visitor refused.

With a lifting of his eyebrows, he asked, "I come to see how you have settled in." His English was good, for he had studied overseas.

"Quite well, actually. I feel already as if I have been here for months."

"Are you getting enough food?"

"Yes. Old Su does a good job."

"He has to, as the students can afford to pay so little. But it can't be enough for you. You must come for a meal with us some time. How was the service on Sunday?"

"Not bad. We had two American families, a teacher from the seminary and a few Chinese students."

"That is good. I would like to take an English service but my English is too bad."

"Not at all. I think it is quite good."

James Yang refused to take this as a compliment. "Not good enough for taking a service. By the way, you must come and preach for us some time. Our service is at 9.30 so there is plenty of time to get back. Our people like to hear you."

"Yes, I would be happy to do that."

"And remember, if there is any way I can help you, you've only to ask. How about the students in the hostel?"

"We have filled all 20 places and there is another student who would like to move in. A third of them are Christians. They all seem to be easy to get on with."

"They are very thrilled to have a foreigner here. I am sure you will have good relation ships. And your teaching in the university – how is that?"

"I don't know how much they understand; but they seem to listen well."

"That is good. You have so many responsibilities. I hope it is not too much for you."

"Not at all. I rather enjoy it."

"That is good. You are a clever man and we are delighted to have you here. And if ever you need help with anything, do come and ask me."

"It is kind of you to offer."

"I mean it. And now for you there is only one thing missing."

"And what is that?"

"A wife. You need a companion. It is not good to be alone."

That was typical of Asians. They could not understand how a person could stay unmarried and yet feel fulfilled. It was not the first time he had had a conversation like this. He recalled his recent discussion with the students. "I am sure that if the Lord wants me to be married he will show me the right person."

"There is a nice girl at the seminary. I feel sure she make a good wife."

"Yang Mushr, I think I should be able to make up my own mind."

"Just trying to help."

They continued to talk for a few more minutes, after which his visitor said he had to attend a church meeting. Left to himself, Peter smiled at all this concern for his own welfare.

It was the next morning when the letter came from Cynthia, telling him that she would like to come on a visit. He wondered what lay behind the request.

24

When Robert came into the shop, Arnold could see that he had something important to say.

"I just had some news," he announced.

"Then you had better share it."

"Have you got time?"

"As you can see, there are no customers right now, and the rest of the stocktaking can wait. Go ahead."

"It's about my job. You know I enjoy going out with the book van, but I have been looking for something more permanent."

"And you've found something?"

"Yes. A while ago I applied to Campus Crusade for student work, but they could not find a place for me. However, I have just heard that one of the men appointed has suddenly withdrawn, and they have asked me to fill his place."

"That is good news for you. Where will you be working?"

"In Taichung. It means I shall have to find somewhere to live; but I have an aunt there who will put me up until I find a place of my own."

"And when do you start?"

"As soon as I can get myself up there. I'm sorry to let you down. It's just ---"

"You're not letting me down. I knew you were only helping me out while you looked for a proper job. No, I'm very happy for you."

This response made Robert a lot more cheerful. "Then I will go this week. Are you sure you can find someone else to go out with the book van?"

"Don't worry about that. It shouldn't be too difficult."

After Robert had left, Arnold pondered his own position. Robert would have the excitement of doing evangelistic work among students and of giving training to new Christians. It sounded much more exciting than helping at a bookshop. He had to admit that he sometimes wondered if he was in the right job. There was never anything very exciting to put in the prayer letters that they sent home.

At that moment a woman came in to choose a Bible, and he offered her a choice among various editions. As she was leaving, to his surprise, Kathleen appeared with little Sammy in his push chair. Philip would be at the kindergarten in the seminary grounds, where he was one of only three white children. Sammy was sucking a lollipop.

"This is a pleasant surprise," he said.

"I thought I'd call round and drop a letter in which came after you left."

She handed it to him and he looked at the sending address. It was from his brother Conor. "He doesn't often write," Kathleen said, "so I thought it might be something important."

He tore the letter open and began to read.

"Well," Kathleen asked. His frown must have alerted her.

"It's bad news. It's about my cousin Keith."

"Do I know him?"

"I don't think so. As you know, we're a big family and it's hard to keep up with everyone."

"You said it was bad news."

"Yes, he was killed in an IRA explosion."

Kathleen gasped. "I'm so sorry. Did it just happen?"

"This letter was posted on Thursday. It happened the day before."

"What are you going to do about it?"

"Write a letter of condolence. I don't see there is much else I can do."

"I know it's hard to be so far away at a time like this."

"Sure it is. And I don't like my brother's insinuation either. He's suggesting that I have a nice soft option here away from all the troubles."

"It's not your fault you're in this position. We both felt led to come to Taiwan long before the troubles began."

"But that doesn't make it any easier. I could've been still back there in Belfast covering the troubles for the local rag. It might've been dangerous at times. But, at least, I wouldn't have been accused of running away."

"Arnold, we both know why we are here. Nobody could accuse us of running away."

"I know; but sometimes it seems wrong to be leading such an easy life here while the rest of the family is living in that tough situation."

"Do you ever feel you are being led back again?"

"No, I don't think so. I suppose I'll get over this; but I would really like some clear demonstration that I am in the place where God wants to use me, sure I would."

BOOK TWO : AUGUST 1951.

25

Until the new red model came into the shop, bicycles were all the same as far as Rose was concerned. Throughout her short life, she could never imagine her father in any other place than the bicycle shop, his hands smudged with oil, happily engaged in repair work. On Sunday afternoon he would take to the roads on his own bicycle to return about eight o'clock (earlier on dark winter days) glowing from the exercise and demanding that his ravenous appetite be satisfied. There was not a lane within 20 miles of Blackburn with which he was not familiar, yet each outing had for him the air of fresh exploration. When she talked with him on other subjects, he was a poor conversationalist, but when the subject turned to bicycles he was in his element. But to the little girl who adored him, bicycles were nothing to get excited about – until the new red Hercules appeared in the shop.

As soon as she saw it, she knew it was for her. Several times her father had suggested getting hold of a second hand machine for her, but her mother, who had a tendency to be over-protective, had exercised the right of veto.

With her twelfth birthday coming up, however, it could no longer be argued that she was too young to go out on the roads. Rose spoke of her wishes time and time again. She became rather anxious, lest some other child should step into the shop and claim it.

It was not as if she was even young in appearance. In fact, she was developing more quickly physically than other members of her class, and this proved a bit of an embarrassment. But, at least, she could play on her maturity to gain her parents' approval for her scheme.

That day her dad was just screwing a new saddle into place when she approached him. "Dad," she began timidly. When he did not appear to hear, she said it again.

"Why, Rosie," he said, looking round. "A didn't 'ear ye come in. Now, wot's up?"

"Dad, it's about the bike."

"T'red one? A saw ye lookin' at it."

"Yes. Couldn't I 'ave it? I'm big enough, and I can ride Johnny 'Olden's."

"Can ye now?" he chortled. "Well, fancy that."

"Ye know it's me birthday soon. I'll be 12. I'm practically a teenager, Dad."

"A know. 'Ard to believe. Ye've grown up so fast."

"Couldn't I 'ave it for me birthday? I could put me pocket money towards it."

He stroked his chin, leaving a trace of oil, as if pondering a weighty problem. "This one's worth quite a bit, ye know, and we're not made of money."

"Oh Dad!"

"A'll 'ave to think about it."

"That's what you always say."

"Yer Mum and I'll 'ave a little talk about it, ok? "

The conversation was at an end. Over the next few days, with no answer forthcoming, Rose dreaded the opening of the shop door, just in case somebody else was coming to claim her beloved machine.

The day of her birthday dawned. At the breakfast table a little pile of cards was waiting for her. Her younger sister Ethel looked rather enviously at her. "Open them, love," her mother encouraged. They were from all the usual people; but her mind was on other things. The more the meal proceeded, the deeper grew her fear that she would be given a book or a game that she didn't want. Dad casually buttered his second slice of toast and Mum poured herself a third cup of tea.

As the meal drew to a close, Dad looked at his watch. "Time to open the shop". He got up from the table. "Oh Rose," he said, "come into the shop for a moment. There's summat A want ye to do."

Dutifully she obeyed. As she entered the shop, her heart missed a beat. The red bicycle was gone! Who could have bought it? As she imagined somebody else riding her bicycle, she could not keep the tears from her eyes. Her father scribbled something on a sheet and handed it to her. "Tek this to Mr and Mrs Threlfall at number 47."

"Yes, Dad."

She was used to running messages. The Threlfalls were very good customers. Though in their fifties, they were both keen cyclists and their bicycles were always spotlessly clean.

As she walked, she tried to blink the tears from her eyes. On arrival, she knocked at the door. Mrs. Threlfall opened it, wiping her hands on a towel as she did so. "My Dad asked me to give you this note."

A smile crept over Mrs. Threlfall's face. She took the note and then fixed Rose with her eyes. Did you read it?"

"No. The note was for you."

"Good girl. Then I'll read it for you. It says, 'Please pass on goods to bearer'. Do you know what goods it means?" Rose shook her head.

Just then Mr. Threlfall appeared in the hallway with a shining red bike. Rose stared opened mouthed. "My bicycle!" she exclaimed.

"That's right," Mr. Threlfall said. It really is yours. Happy birthday.!"

She stuttered her thanks, but Mrs. Threlfall said, "Don't thank us. Thank your parents. We were just keeping it for you as a surprise."

"Can you ride it, love?" Mr. Threlfall asked.

"Yes, I've practised on Sally Ogden's bike. And I can even ride Johnny 'Olden's. 'Onest. I know what to do. I'll show you."

Lovingly she wheeled the bicycle down the hall, through the garden and out on to the road. She mounted, and, after a few wobbles, managed to pursue an even course in the direction of home. She thought of waving, but that might upset her balance and give a bad impression.

When she got home she thanked her parents profusely. Her father hinted that he might even allow her to accompany him on one of his weekly expeditions, but her mother looked somewhat apprehensive about this, and said something about the need to take care.

That same afternoon, she asked if she might go on a practice run. Her parents consented, though her mother suggested that she should not go far.

As she set out, she reflected on the new horizons that now extended before her. Instead of confining herself to Audley Range, she would be able to venture to much more distant places. The world was at her feet.

At the crossroads she had a choice. She could either turn right and cycle downhill into town; or she could turn left and take a steep climb would would bring her out to the countryside. She decided on the second course.

The biggest challenge was Brandy House Brow. To cycle up such a steep incline was impossible even for the most seasoned cyclist. As she pushed her bicycle up the slope, it seemed to get steadily heavier. At last, beside the well-named 'Stop and Rest' inn, she paused for a breather. After a slight incline, she found herself poised for a downward run into Lower Darwen. This was new terrain for her.

She remounted and delighted in the freedom of this easy run. Already she was in an area of open fields. A breeze wafted against her cheeks. The edges became a green blur. She could go on like this for weeks, maybe years.

Gradually, however, she became aware that she was travelling too fast. She applied the brakes. There was a jerk and she began to wobble. She applied the brakes once more, with the same result. Suddenly the world appeared to do a somersault.

Fortunately the motorist who stopped for her was driving a capacious station wagon. It was not difficult to find room for the buckled machine and the bruised rider. When her mother opened the door and saw her in the arms of a stranger, she looked as if she was ready to collapse.

It was decided that, there being no broken limbs, bed rest and frequent cups of tea would have the required effect. When delivering the third cup, Mum sat on the bed and looked at her with a hint of reprimand in her eyes. "And now, my girl, " she said, "we're going to mek sure that you never go so far from 'ome again!" Little did she know....

26

Alleyne swung round the bend in her old black saloon. After a somewhat tiring deputation trip, she was glad to be home at last. There was the sign 'White Springs'. This small Colorado township was becoming more familiar to her, but it would never feel like home. The population stood at around 600 and the number of buildings, though scattered, did not exceed 200.

For news of births, marriages and deaths, it was not necessary to consult a newspaper, for news soon got round by word of mouth. She had been here for six months now, staying with her brother and his wife, ever since the Communists had forced her out of southern China.

She still shuddered when she thought of those days in prison – the grey walls that fenced her in, the large brown cockroaches which crawled over her in the night, the hours of interrogation in that white-walled room that had once been a doctor's surgery, the constant accusations. If she had not had the assurance that she was suffering for the Lord's sake, she could never have borne it. Then came the sudden and unexpected release, the long train journey to Hong Kong, the effusive welcome from her associates there and the glorious sense of freedom.

Her only surviving relative was her brother Stanley, who operated a gas station in this little community. His wife, Jessica, had given the impression that three was a crowd and reminded her frequently that this arrangement was only temporary. Stanley was a good handyman, and he converted a space at the back of the house so that she could use it as her apartment and maintain some measure of independence. Of course, this was only for a little while; and Alleyne hoped that one day she would be able to return to her beloved China. If this should not prove possible, then she hoped she would be able to work amongst Chinese people elsewhere in the East.

Her society had put her on deputation work. Most weekends, therefore, she was away from home, fulfilling her speaking engagements. On these occasions she spoke graphically of life under the Communists and held people in thrall, but sometimes it was hard to do so without a tear in her eye. Although she prided herself on her self-control, even she was touched by emotions at times.

When she was not speaking elsewhere, she attended the little Baptist church just down the road. The minister was a 40 year old widower, Rev. Merlin Katz, who was cared for by his sister Marge. Originally a Denver man, he had laboured in this community for seven years and was much liked by the members of his congregation. In fact, she had an invitation to eat at his home that evening.

Her brother was just filling a customer's gas tank. He waved at her as she stepped out of the car. Alleyne was glad she had her own key to the apartment, and she quietly let herself in. There was a pile of letters waiting to be read, but there was one which particularly attracted her attention. It was from her mission.

She tore open the envelope and sat down to read it. After much thought and prayer, they had come up with a possible new post for her. There was a Bible School in Formosa that was looking for a new teacher. Was she interested? If so, it was proposed to send her to a local Bible School for a semester to get some training, with a view to going out in the early Spring.

Formosa! That was the nearest thing to being on the Mainland of China. The prospect excited her. To be a teacher would be right up her street. She could not have asked for a better offer. Nevertheless, she needed to pray for a bit about it. If she made a mistake at this point, she might have to live with it for a long time.

She told her brother a little later as they shared a cup of tea in his part of the house. "That's great news," he said. "You always were more Chinese than American – not like me, I'm afraid. You would be able to eat Chinese food again instead of eating our stuff here. It would be just as if you had never left China."

"Not quite. I'm sure it must be very different in Formosa from what I was used to, but it's the next best thing. We shall even have the same President – Chiang Kai Shek."

"Will you take the job?"

"Probably; but I still need to pray about it."

Jessica came into the room and they shared the news with her. She was enthusiastic about it, but Alleyne wondered whether the main reason for this was that they would not have to share their house any more.
She spent a while opening the other letters, but there was nothing else as dramatic as this one. Yes, she had spent long

enough in this quiet place that did not feel like home, and could not wait to get back into a Chinese environment.

That evening she went as planned to the minister's home. The door was opened by his sister, Marge, a dumpy woman with a florid complexion.

"Am I too early?" she asked.

"No, you're just right. Merlin's in the study. You'll excuse me if I just finish the preparations."

Merlin, hearing the voices, came out to greet her. He had a habit of wearing his spectacles on the end of his nose, and she kept wanting to push them into a safer position. "Would you like a Coke?" he asked.

"No thanks. Not for me. I never did like it."

"Then you won't mind if I take a drop?"

He poured some out and it fizzed and popped in the glass. "I find it has some comfort value. Ever since Beth died I've been looking for other comforts. I know I ought to find all my comfort in the Lord, but I find I need other little comforts too."

"It must've been very hard for you."

"It has. Not a day goes by when I don't miss her. We did everything together – well, almost everything."

"Yes, I suppose it must've been very difficult for you when you had been so close."

"I don't suppose you've ever had such a close relationship with anyone, Alleyne."

"I was close to my parents when we all lived in China together; but I've learned to be independent. I've got the Lord, and that's what keeps me going."

"Yes, I can see that." he poured himself more of this dark liquid. "Have you never felt in need of a close companion?"

"They sometimes put new workers to live with me, but we didn't get on. Our ideas were so different."

"I meant someone really close. Never had a romance?"

"Oh, Mr. Katz, how can you say such a thing? I'm not that kind of person. When I'm doing the Lord's work I don't have time for other things."

"But your situation has changed so much. That work in China is behind you, and you are ready for a different future."

It was at this point that Alleyne became aware of where the conversation was leading. She must squash this conversation before it became more intolerable. Marriage was not a part of her planning. Yet just for a moment she saw the situation through his eyes. He was a lonely man, devastated by the loss of his wife and longing for a new companion. She, Alleyne, was close at hand and apparently available and had closed the door on one phase of her life ready to start another. She might even seem physically attractive to a man in his position, though she herself had never been concerned about her self image. Just for a moment she could picture herself living in this house and sharing in the ministry of this man whom she greatly respected. But it was only for a moment. Had not God made it clear to her that hers was to be a solitary path? Others needed companionship, but she was above that. And, in any case, she belonged among the Chinese.

"I think there is something you should know," she said.

"Oh, and what is that, Alleyne?"

"I got a letter this morning. It was from the mission. They have openings for some of their former China workers in Formosa, and they have invited me to teach in a seminary there."

"I see." This news did not exactly fill him with joy. Because of this, Alleyne's suspicions were confirmed.

"And what is your reaction to this?"

"It seems to me like an opening given by God. He knows I 've given my life to the Chinese people, and this is a chance to continue."

"There are Chinese people in Formosa?"

"Of course. It is a breakaway from the Mainland. Sometimes they call it Taiwan. They speak Mandarin and their local language as well, which happens to be the same language I used in Fuchien province when I was growing up. It is a God-given opportunity."

"I see. I had hoped --- "

"Yes, I have some idea of what you had hoped: that is why I have to speak openly and honestly."

"And I respect you for it. It was foolish of me to think - "

"God will provide someone who can be a much better companion to you than I could ever be."

"I would like to think so."

She laid her hand on his. It was not the sort of thing she would normally do, but she sensed that for a moment this man needed a crumb of comfort.

Madge appeared at the door. "Ready for you both."

It had been a definitive moment. Now she was committed to a life of living alone amongst the Chinese people.

27

School was over for the day. Swinging his satchel, twelve year old Peter emerged from the grey stone building into the sunshine. Here in Keswick, rain was more common, but today the clouds had rolled back. On such a day it would be a more attractive proposition to go walking in the hills.

He strolled together with his new friend, Geoffrey Coppitt, a boy slightly stockier than himself, who managed to maintain a cheerful grin in all circumstances.

"Peter, how about coming to my house for a bit?" he invited.

Peter thought for a moment. His mother would probably be so immersed in a book of poems that she would not be aware that it was time for him to return. His father would still be in afternoon surgery and would not miss him. "Yes, I'd like to," he replied.

It was an uphill walk. After being cooped up in school all day, they welcomed the exercise. As they walked they discussed the French lesson from which they had just emerged and agreed that the test had been too difficult. Even though Peter was good at languages, this had been a challenge.

The Coppitt house was set back a little from the road. There was a long drive. The grass in the garden was long, but one could just make out what was meant to be flower borders, where a few marigolds and nasturtiums struggled for existence. "We don't seem to get a lot of time for gardening," Geoffrey explained. "We're quite a big family. There's – well, you can see for yourself when we get inside."

Instead of taking him through the front door, Geoffrey escorted him to the back of the house and they entered through the kitchen door.

Mrs. Coppitt was busy, like a major with his troops, commanding the affairs of the kitchen. A large pan had been set on the stove. On the table was a huge mixing bowl, and, with vigorous movements of the arm, she was stirring some undefined mixture. She was one of the biggest women Peter had ever seen, but when he saw her ample face Peter knew where Geoffrey got his smile from.

"So you're back, are you?" Mrs. Coppitt bent and planted a juicy kiss on Geoffrey's forehead. Peter was a little taken aback, as this was not normal practice at home; but was relieved to find that this treatment was not extended to visitors.

"This is my friend Peter Falconer," Geoffrey explained.

"Good to see you, Peter. Any friend of Geoffrey's is welcome in this house." It seemed that the mixture was ready, for she turned it out into two trays. "Let me see, you must be the doctor's boy."

"Yes. How did you know?"

"Not many people round here called Falconer. And anyway, you look a bit like him. Are you thinking of following that line?"

"I don't know. I mean, it's early days yet."

"Of course it is. Much too early to bother about things like that. Second shelf."

The last remark was addressed to Geoffrey, who was looking for something in the refrigerator. He took out a jug and began to pour orangeade into two glasses. "Here are the biscuits."

Somehow Mrs. Coppitt managed to find a free hand to render this assistance.

"Hey, don't put them back!" This cry came from a pigtailed schoolgirl who had just come into the room. She seized a glass and helped herself.

"This is Janice," Geoffrey explained. Peter thought he had seen her around but she was probably still in primary school. "I'll show you the house," Geoffrey volunteered. Still clutching his glass, Peter followed. Geoffrey led him into a room that was cluttered with toys. There was a one-eared teddy bear, a rocking horse with the red paint peeling, a compendium of board games, railway lines and a little black engine, a bookcase full of children's books, a metal spinning top, toy soldiers drawn up for battle, an alarm clock with the works hanging out, a large football and a pair of roller skates. In one corner there stood a large rocking chair. "That's where we used to go when we were frightened," he said. "Mum would sit there and rock us. Of course, we've got past that now. But when Dad comes back from work he sits and reads us a story. Mainly for the younger kids, but Janice and I still enjoy it, even though we can read for ourselves."

Peter could not remember when his father had last read him a story. He was always too busy for such things.

Suddenly an Indian chief, who had been hiding in a corner, leaped out to attack them. Unmoved by the ferocity of the assailant, Geoffrey announced that this was Tommy and that he was four. "You won't see Brian," he added. "He's working, and Bella got married last year. She lives in Cockermouth, but sometimes comes over on Sundays."

The conducted tour continued. The house was by no means as big as his own, but it was obviously a place where people felt content. Behind the house there was a big rambling garden. Geoffrey showed him a house in a tree. "Dad made that for me. Want to come up?"

Peter's family had a big garden too. The grass was always neatly cut, for they employed a man to do it, and the flowerbeds were always carefully weeded and planted. It seemed to Peter that here was a family that knew how to live, whereas at his own place they were simply existing.

It was nearly time to leave. Mrs. Coppitt was just taking a pie from the oven. It smelt delicious. "You must come and eat with us one of these days," she suggested. "Ask your Mum and Dad when they will let you come and tell Geoffrey at school. Any time will be right for us."

Slowly Peter walked back to his own home. He hoped that one day in the future he would marry and start a home of his own. He wanted it to be a happy place, with family members who knew how to enjoy one another.

He came to the familiar double gate and to the brass plate which read "Reginald Falconer", with a host of letters after it. He walked up the neat path and let himself in quietly, taking care to wipe his feet thoroughly on the mat.

There was a smell of burning. From the kitchen came his mother's voice. "Is that you, Peter?" When he entered the kitchen he saw that she was attempting to remove something from the oven which had originally been intended as their evening meal. Maybe now it would be a tin of cold meat instead. On the table, as if put down in haste, there was a slim volume of poems by a writer called Hopkins.

He was home.

28

Arnold was coming to the conclusion that journalism was not all that it was cracked up to be. Day after day he found himself writing trivial articles for trivial people.

This particular assignment was a good example. His task was to go to the Belfast Royal Infirmary, where a mother had just given birth to her baby son. This is itself was of not great significance, but there was one thing which made this different from other births.

The nurse was kind enough to draw a curtain round the bed so that they could enjoy some measure of privacy. He explained the reason for his coming. The new mother was a chubby, fresh faced woman, whose face lit up when he introduced himself.

"Honoured, I'm sure," she said. "How they got to know about it I don't rightly know, but it's very unnerstanding of 'em to send you here. Glad to tell you anything you want to know, sure I am."

"It's about the baby."

"Course it is. If it weren't about the babby you wouldn't be here, would you?"

"I gather he was born today."

"Just after 2 o'clock this morning. He wasn't due till the 15th, but he came early. I knew he would. My husband's a keen Orangeman and there's a march today. I think junior wanted to celebrate that, sure he did."

"So that's why you gave him that special name."

"Aye, that's it: King Billy."

"But don't you think that King Billy is rather a strange name to give a child?"

"Not at all. We all has a lot of respect for King Billy. He stands for our Loyalist cause. What better name could I give him?"

"Would it not have been better to have called him just 'Billy'?"

"Not at all. Billys are two a penny. But not all are called <u>King</u> Billy."

"Don't you think it will be a bit of an embarrassment to him when he grows up?"

"Why should it? If he's a good Protestant, he should be proud of it."

"Let us hope so."

"I thought you was here from the paper to tell folks about it. What are you doing stirring things up?"

"I'm sorry. I just thought it strange, that's all."

"Maybe you're a Catholic."

"Not at all."

"Then what's your problem?" She went on:"I wouldn't be surprised if we don't get a lot of folk who like the idea. Make sure you give us a good write-up. Front page an' all."

He was going to say something about Protestants and Catholics burying their differences, but he could see that his words would have fallen on stony ground. Instead he said, "Is there anything else you would like to tell our readers?"

"No, you've got it all, haven't you? Make sure you get it right. And now, if you don't mind, I'd like to rest a wee bit."

It irked him that he would have to write an article on this interview that was unbiased. Instead of calling her an implacable bigot, he would just have to tell the facts plainly. Anything more than that could cost him his job. He was not free to be himself: he simply had to reflect the world in which he lived.

He nursed this grievance when sitting by the fireside with his father that evening. The latter, balding rapidly, was puffing away at the pipe without which he was rarely seen. "When you took on this job," he said, "you had some idea what you were letting yourself in for. This is Northern Ireland, sure it is, and ye'll never get people all seeing eye to eye. If you'd been working for one of them Lunnon papers, you could've been sent to Vietnam or somewhere where there's a lot of action, but when you work for a Belfast newspaper you have to put up with the local situation, whatever you may think about it."

"No one would send me that far at my age."

"I know that, son, but it could happen one day. Who knows?"

"But it's all so trivial. Half the stuff I have to write about is all about people's prejudices."

"In Northern Ireland, prejudice is news. Let's face it."

"I hate prejudice. I may be a good Protestant, but that does not mean I should take a dig at the other side."

"If you were working at Short's like me you wouldn't have any problem. You would have a good steady job, and a chance of promotion."

"But don't you understand, Pop, that's not what I want. I don't want a good steady job. I want my life to count."

There was a pause while his father tried to relight his pipe. "I'm satisfied with my life, son," he said at length. I've made a good contribution to production and that's enough for me."

"But I'm not made the same way as you are, Pop. I can't go through the same routine every day. Don't you see that? I sometimes wonder whether I should get a job overseas."

"And what about us?" his mother ventured as she came bustling into the room. "Worrying ourselves stiff in case you get blown up by a bomb or eaten by tigers."

"Oh, Mum, you always have to be so dramatic. Just because you read about some occasional trouble in the newspapers it doesn't mean that as soon as you set foot outside the UK you're in trouble."

"That's what it sounds like. Here's a nice place to be. You can't beat the Irish countryside."

"What about the IRA?"

"Just a few boys playing games," his mother said. "Nobody takes them seriously these days."

"I can maybe pull a few strings to get you in at Short's," his father said.

"But I don't want to work there. I want to be more independent."

"Independent? Being forced to write articles about things you object to?"

"It's a start. It won't always be like this."

"How do you know?"

"I was reading something the other day," his mother went on as she poked the fire. "It was about making the most of the present. It said that instead of wondering what you were going to do in the future you should work hard at what you are doing at the moment. Seemed like good advice to me."

"I try to do a good job right now," Arnold responded, "but that doesn't mean I can't make plans as well."

"Anyhow," his mother continued, "let's not have any more talk of leaving us. At least, you've got a good job, a respectable one, and that's more than can be said for some people these days."

His father picked up his newspaper as a sign that he no longer wished to be a part of the conversation.

Arnold retired to his room, a small box room, where he could be alone for a while. Could he really live like this for long? Surely there was somewhere in the world where he could satisfy his longing for excitement. One day his opportunity would come. There was also the question of how his Christian faith entered into all this. It was not just a matter of finding overseas work that excited him but of going somewhere where he could live out his faith in a meaningful and satisfying way. What he needed was divine guidance.

BOOK THREE: FEBRUARY-MARCH 1972

29

The Chinese New Year celebrations were over, and life was getting back to normal. The schools and colleges had two terms annually – one before the holiday and one after. The students were trickling back in order to be ready for the new term. Rose liked to be around in order to welcome them back and to deal with any queries they might have.

At the moment, however, she was engaged in another task that had nothing to do with her work. She was preparing the guest room for a special visitor. When she heard that Peter's girl friend was coming over from England and that Peter was reluctant to house her at St. John's lest this should be misunderstood, she offered the use of the seminary guest room. Peter had accepted the proposal gladly, and the college authorities were perfectly happy with the suggestion.

Now it was time to make the bed, to lay out towels and to ensure that the place was habitable. Even now Peter would be in Taipei meeting her off her plane at Sung Shan Airport. In the months since his arrival, she had got to know Peter better. Like herself, he had a very caring attitude toward his students. He was a little more bookish than she was, but in general they were fond of the same things. It was foolish, though, to muse over this. She was still fighting against the assumption others had made that she would throw herself at the first eligible bachelor to come her way. Having entered upon missionary work in the knowledge that, in all likelihood, this would mean remaining single, and she was still prepared for this probability. In a way, she welcomed Cynthia's visit. It was clear to everyone that this was Peter's girl friend and could well end up as his marriage partner. In the light of this, nobody would be trying to throw Peter and herself together. They could remain casual friends and members of the same fellowship group, but there was nothing more than that. It felt safe.

That morning she had heard that, because of a sore back, her father was giving up the cycle shop. It had been so much a part of his life that it was hard to know how he would spend his time. It would, at least, give her parents more quality time together. The shop would become a hardware store. That was hard to imagine. Her parents expected to move to a flat, as they only had themselves to look after. Home would never be quite the same again. But that was not the only news. Ethel's second child had been born – a little girl called Tammy. Now they were a family of four. If only....

She was musing on this as she left the building and headed across the courtyard, and almost collided with Florence. "Why, I did not see you there."

Florence dropped her books. As they were picking them up again she said: "I just got back."

"Did you have a good holiday?"

"Very good. I spent a lot of time with my parents and my brother. We ate lots of food. We also spent time with an uncle I had not seen for a long time."

"Yes, it is always a great family occasion, like our Christmas in the West. Most people should be back by now. Is Catherine back yet?"

A look of puzzlement crossed Florence's face. "She has not come back. I think there is a problem."

"What sort of a problem?"

"She sent me a letter. She said she did not think she would be able to come back."

"Why not? I thought that she had got over her mother's death in November and was coping rather well."

"Yes, it was all very sad. I know that Catherine loved her mother and she misses her a lot."

"But that is no reason to leave the college; unless it is because of lack of finance."

"She did not say why."

"But I still don't understand the reason for her not coming back. I thought we had given her some financial help."

"We did. Sz Lausu arranged that. Money is not a problem, now."

"Then why is she not coming back?"

"Maybe she will come after all."

"You're sure she didn't say what the problem was?"

"She didn't say anything. It was as if she were afraid of something."

"Afraid of what? I wish I could see her and talk about this. I thought she was enjoying her course at college."

"Oh yes, she enjoyed it very much. I know she was happy here most of the time. I don't know what is wrong."

"I'd like to be able to talk with her about this."

"You could go to see her."

"It is hard to get to her village by public transport."

"I know. She has to walk for miles."

"But you did not say she would definitely not be coming back."

"No, I didn't. Maybe she will come back after all."

As she continued on her way, Rose thought more upon this matter. The problem that had plagued Catherine earlier had been solved. What had gone wrong now? She could not help worrying about this. It was a part of her nature to be worried too much about other people's problems.

30

Even though they had been friends for some time, it was the first time Alleyne and Helen had eaten together at Helen's home. It was not the first time, however, that Alleyne had visited the place, and, getting off the bus, she had walked a hundred yards down the road, turned up a narrower road, and then followed the little track to the house itself. Just in front of the house there was a square pit filled with water. It was difficult to think of any useful purpose it might serve: indeed, it might prove a big hazard to traffic or even to the unwary pedestrian.

Helen had greeted her with a pot of Chinese tea. They had no interest in that Western custom of drinking sherry. Meanwhile, Mr. Yu, the cook, was putting the finishing touches to the food preparation. At length he put his head round the door and said, "Haule".

"Forgive me for not preparing something myself," Helen said. "It is so convenient having Mr. Yu to do this for me, especially after a tiring day at the school."

"I quite understand," Alleyne remarked. "I usually eat with the students. It saves a lot of trouble." A thought suddenly occurred to her. "You must come and eat with the rest of us some time."

"I would be delighted. Now shall we eat?"

They moved into the kitchen and sat on stools at a table

covered with a plastic cloth. Alleyne approved of these simple
arrangements. The food provided was sour bean soup, a beef
and vegetable dish and a dish that included squid,
accompanied, of course, by rice.

"I just have Mr. Yu for five days a week," she said. "I do my
own cooking at weekends; but it is such a long way to go to the
shops."

"I know. I'm surprised that you stick it out here. It would be
much more convenient if you lived a bit nearer the town centre.
Nearer the school would be a good idea."

"I like it here because it's nice and quiet."

"That's for sure. Don't you ever get lonely?"

"Not really. I like my own company."

"Just as well you do."

"I still enjoy our little outings. Then there are always plenty of
people around me at the school. But it's always good to get
back here."

Alleyne's attention was caught by a black and white portrait of
a stern-looking woman on the wall. She assumed that it was
Helen's mother, and must have been taken a long time ago.

Helen observed her reaction. "That was my mother, as I
suppose you have guessed. She ruled my sister and me with an
iron hand; but, at least, it taught us some manners and some

discipline."

"I wonder what she would have thought if she had known you were coming here."

"I don't think she would have understood at all. She belonged to her own time. Our ancestors lived in the same village generation after generation. I am the first one to break out of the mould; but, then, times have changed so much."

"Is your sister married?"

"Yes, and she has three children. So, at least someone is keeping the family line going. What about yours?"

"Just a brother, and he has one son who helps him at the gas station."

"So nobody is looking to you to continue the family line."

"Not at all."

"Did you never think of marrying?"

"There was a slight possibility once, but it did not come to anything. I feel I made the right decision."

"Yes, I can't imagine either of us being a family person."

At this point in the conversation Mr. Yu, the cook, came into the room. Helen thanked him for the meal, and he said "Nali", which was the polite thing to say in such circumstances. He looked to be a lonely figure, Alleyne surmised, and hard to get to know. How Helen tolerated him she did not know. She felt there was something shifty about him.

When he was gone, Helen said, "You don't mind if we do the washing up ourselves? He will have done the big things."

"No problem. How long has he been working for you?"

"Nearly twelve months."

"And you find him reliable?"

"Of course. Otherwise I would send him packing. I know he is not exactly a charmer, but it takes all sorts."

"I suppose he's glad to earn a bit of money. Does he have a family?"

"He never speaks of family. I think he lives alone."

"That's unusual for a Chinese."

"I think he has family back in Mainland China; but, of course, no contact is permitted."

When they had cleared their plates, Helen asked: "Would you like some ice cream?"

"Not for me, thanks. I eat simply."

"Then you won't mind if I have a little myself?"

As Helen was helping herself to this, Alleyne said, "You said you are a long way from the shops. I don't know how you can keep it frozen on your long walk back."

"There is one shop just round the corner. It comes in handy."

"And your nearest bank must be a couple of miles away."

"Yes. That is why I keep my money in the house."

"Is that wise?"

"I don't tell people about it. And it is carefully hidden."

"I should hope so. But it still doesn't seem to be very wise."

"I am very careful about it."

"You will need to be."

"However, that's enough about me. What about you?"

"What do you mean? How I look after my money?"

"No, about your job. You said a while ago that it was not secure."

"That's right. No verdict yet, but I expect I will hear more soon."

"I do hope they let you stay on. I would be lost without you."

"If I have to leave, I guess I don't know what I shall do. Of course, it is for my society to come up with something."

"Have they said anything?" Her eyes were full of concern.

"They can't say anything yet until the principal has made up his mind. I expect to hear shortly whether there will still be a job for me or not."

"It seems so ungrateful to cast you off like that when you have given faithful service for such a long time."

"I know, but the situation is beyond my control. When I get some definite words about my future, I shall be able to discuss the matter with my society."

Helen finished her dessert and they carried their dishes into the kitchen. While Helen began to fill the sink with hot water, Alleyne took up a tea towel.

"I hope they find something for you here in Nancheng. I would miss you if you went away."

"What I would really like is to be able to return to China, but that is out of the question at the moment. We don't get much information right now out of China because of this terrible Cultural Revolution. I hope the day will come when missionaries can return, but the situation is very bleak at the moment."

"Sadly," Helen remarked, "I have never been there, and it does not look as if I ever shall."

When the washing up was completed, Alleyne looked at her watch. "I think I had better be getting back. Someone will be missing me."

"Who?" A look of puzzlement crossed Helen's face.

"Why, Sandy, of course."

31

Peter was waiting at the Arrivals area of Sung Shan Airport. Many of those who came out were Americans, wheeling large amounts of luggage. It was fascinating just to study each person and try to understand the personal background.

Soon it would be time for Cynthia to emerge. He still could not believe that she was willing to make such a long journey. How did he really feel about her? Was this the opportunity to renew their commitment to one another? Or would it confirm that suspicion now long held, that their ways must part for good? Peter knew there was no way of predicting how all this was going to turn out.

Just when there was a lull in the number of passengers emerging, she appeared, tall, aquiline and pale for that setting, with that same lock of brown hair drooping over her left eye, still wearing the heavy coat which she must have needed when setting out, and pulling a large case which looked as if it must have seriously challenged the weight restrictions on checking in. She looked a little bewildered, but her eyes lit up when she saw him.

They exchanged a hug. "Smooth journey?" he asked.

"It was much too long," she complained. "I wish you had chosen to live somewhere nearer home."

"It was brave of you to make such a long journey."

"The girls at work said I was a fool even to try it. They didn't think I had it in me, and I proved them wrong."

"So you did. And are you glad you made the effort?"

"I'll tell you when I've been here a bit longer."

Peter took hold of her case handle, whilst she continued to carry her small bag. He informed her: "We're going to take a taxi to the station. It isn't so far."

"Will that be expensive?"

"No, it's nothing like the prices back home."

When they came to the exit, they found a long line of taxis waiting for customers. It was five or six minutes before their turn came. Peter told the driver where they wanted to go. He looked a little disappointed as if he would have preferred them to go to a more distant destination, but it was the rule that, despite their long wait, they must accept the fare which they got. As they started their journey, the driver sought to compensate for his surly beginning by telling Peter how good his Mandarin was. It was a conversation which Peter had had many times before.

"What are you talking about?" Cynthia asked.

"Oh, he is just saying how good he thinks my Chinese is."

"I wouldn't know, would I?" she said ruefully. "I've never been much good at foreign languages."

As they continued on their journey, Cynthia became somewhat apprehensive. "Do they always go so fast?" she asked.

"You get used to it," Peter assured her. "Actually, this is quite slow. By local standards."

She did not see the humour of that remark. It was convenient that the journey was so short. Peter told her that there was talk of building a new airport in a more remote location, which would add a lot of length to journey times.

In due course they came to the station. Peter thanked the driver for his help, but did not leave a tip, as this was the way things were done in Taiwan. There were crowds of people making the way into the station.

"Is this a special holiday?" Cynthia asked.

"No, it's just a normal day. The Chinese New Year is well over. What made you ask?"

"There are so many people."

"It's always like this. You'll soon get used to it."

Staring around her, Cynthia asked, "Where do we buy our tickets?"

"That's all done. If you don't buy your tickets beforehand, you don't get a seat."

"Are they really so busy?"

They were a little early, so Peter took her into a waiting room. He noticed that she looked tired after the long journey. "Maybe I should have booked us in somewhere here in Taipei where you could have got a good night's rest. You must be suffering from jet lag."

"Jet lag. Culture shock. You name it, and I've got it. But I'm quite happy to get to your place tonight and then have a good night's sleep."

"As long as you're happy with that." He felt a bit of the old tenderness coming back into their relationship and he also saw himself as her protector, for the time being, against all that was unfamiliar and even threatening.

"I think it's time to board the train," he told her after a little while.

"You lead me then. I wouldn't know where to go."

He escorted her through the barrier to a train which was white with a long blue stripe. "This is the Ju Guang Hao," he explained.

"I'm sorry, I don't know what you mean."

"There are various types of trains and this is the most luxurious one." As they boarded the train, a girl in a blue uniform saluted them.

She nodded approvingly. "Yes, this does look rather comfortable. Do we sit where we want?"

"No, all the seats are numbered. We are over there in the corner. Numbers 1 and 3."

As they took the seats, she looked around her as the carriage began to fill up. "The men are very well dressed," she commented.

"Yes, the business men usually wear dark suits here. They are the ones who can best afford to take the most expensive train. If we had taken one of the others it would have been a very different experience. If the person beside you had a bag that moved, you could guess that it would be full of chickens."

"Now that would have been an experience." Her mouth curved into a smile. Her initial reaction to the experience was more positive than he had expected. Maybe she would be capable of adapting after all. If so, what did this mean about the future of their relationship? Did they truly love one another? That was the most important thing, and that was what they would need to test over the next few days.

A young steward, carrying a large kettle, lifted each glass, flicked open the lid, and poured water into it with commendable agility. "You'll find there are already tea leaves in the cup," Peter explained.

"So there are. He seems very good at his job."

"He gets plenty of experience. He will keep coming as the journey goes on. The tea gets weaker and weaker, but that is all part of the experience."

The train began to move. "If you feel like sleeping," Peter said, "don't mind me."

"No, I would like to see the scenery. It's all so new to me." Even so, her eyelids were flickering in protest.

So far so good. How would she react to Nancheng, to his friends, and to his living and working environments? It was impossible to predict.

32

"Don't forget next Monday," warned Pastor Fan.

Arnold's mind was a blank. Pastor Fan observed this and explained: " Paul Fennigan – Feng Mushr, we call him. It's the start of the budauhui."

"Oh yes, I'd forgotten. Well, I hadn't really. It's just that I have a lot on my mind."

"You should remember. It will give you opportunity to sell

some books."

"Of course. I'll be there."

"And don't forget to pray for lots of converts," Pastor Fan beamed.

Arnold was glad when the pastor left, and he was able to shut the shop. It had been a long day at the bookstore, and he would be glad to be back home with his family. As he drove home, he was contemplating future trips with the van. This would have to wait until the week of evangelistic meetings finished. Since Robert was no longer with him, on the last four such occasion he had been on his own, and it was not the same. He really needed someone to accompany him on these trips. Recently it had occurred to him that there might be a student at the seminary who would like to earn a little extra money by doing this. He must talk with Rose some time about the possibility.

The best part of coming home was the welcome he got from his sons. On this day the sun was shining, but it was a cool 58 degrees – the family would need to wear coats for walking. After the usual rough and tumble, they set out together before the evening meal. Sammy refused to use the pushchair. What was good enough for Philip was good enough for him. Because of the many obstacles on the pathways and the danger of the open sewers that lined the roads, they clutched the children tightly by the hand.

As a foreign family, they always attracted a lot of attention. The children's golden hair drew a cluster of admirers and people had even been known to pull it in order to see if it was real, a practice which the boys objected to strongly.

As they were passing a small store, Kathleen recalled that they were running out of biscuits, and the family waited while she went in to buy a packet.

No one was quite sure how it happened. There was a sudden cry of panic from Sammy and he vanished into the gutter. The filthy water only went up to his waist, but he seemed to have banged his head on the side, for he was rubbing it and crying. Arnold reacted by yanking him out. The whole family was in a state of shock.

"How does it feel?" Arnold asked him.

"It hurts," Sammy sobbed.

"He needs to go to hospital." Philip pronounced, as if he were himself a parent.

"He's right," Kathleen agreed as she took him up into her arms. "Let's change these trousers, and then we can take a taxi there. You can't be too careful with head injuries."

Fortunately, they had only walked a few yards and it was easy to get back inside and exchange the soiled shorts for clean ones.

There were two or three hospitals in the vicinity, but the obvious choice was Father Smith. It was a Roman Catholic establishment, and reputedly more reliable than the others in the vicinity, though even this one had its limitations. Once a friend of theirs, happily pregnant, had been offered an injection which, had she accepted it, would have taken the baby away. You had to be so careful, even in the more reputable establishments.

They all went together by taxi. Both parents wanted to ensure that little Sammy would get the best of attention, and Philip did not want to be left out of any family affairs.

The casualty department looked a bit chaotic, with small children darting hither and thither, but the waiting time was only about 20 minutes.

They were seen by a tall, thin doctor in a white coat, who told them his name was Chen. Kathleen explained what had happened. Sammy was no longer crying, but he was still snivelling. The doctor spent some time examining him carefully with a rather serious expression, which Arnold and Kathleen hoped did not mean there was bad news.

At length the doctor ended the examination and prepared to comment. "There is no evidence of any serious damage," he pronounced' "but with this sort of thing it is unwise to make quick conclusions. I think we need to keep him here overnight, just in case it is more serious than we think. Probably he will be fine, and we should be able to let him go home in the morning. Are you happy with that? It is just a precaution, nothing more."

"Yes, we would be happy with that," Kathleen said, "but he is a bit young to be left on his own. Would it be possible for one of us to stay here overnight with him?"

"Of course. No problem."

"I think I should do it," Kathleen offered. "Arnold, you could look after Philip at home."

"Is he going to get better?" Philip asked anxiously.

"Of course," Arnold assured him, "and we men will have a great time on our own, won't we just?" He did not feel as confident as he sounded.

33

It was best, Rose reflected, to let Cynthia sleep for as long as she was able. She herself was no stranger to jet lag, and you never really knew how it was going to affect you. These were her thoughts as she sipped her morning coffee. This was a luxury she permitted herself just once a day, for coffee was expensive in Taiwan.

She could see why Peter had been attracted to Cynthia. It was not for her looks, for her pale complexion her plain features and her straightline figure did not make her sexually attractive, but there was a warmth in her character that made you feel you could relate easily to her. She had seemed somewhat ill at ease on their first meeting the previous evening, but that could easily be attributed to the length of her journey and the strangeness of her surroundings. Time would tell whether she was capable of relating to this new environment and making her home here as Peter's wife.

In moments of fantasy, Rose had imagined what it would like for herself to be married to Peter, but she dismissed these thoughts swiftly, as he was potentially committed to someone else, and this was not a current option. Cynthia had enough to get used to without also facing the threat of a rival!
Suddenly there was a knock at the door. She called out a reply and the door opened to reveal Florence with a letter in her hand. "Li Lausu," she cried. "Do you have time?"

"I will always have time for you." That answer sounded a bit mushy, but it was out and could not be retracted. "Sit down. Do you want some coffee?"

"I don't drink coffee, thank you." Rose was about to offer her something else, but she realized that her guest was much more interested in communicating some information than in accepting the courtesies of hospitality.

"Now what is it you wanted to tell me?"

"I just got this letter." She waved the piece of paper in the air as if to prove her point.

"Who is it from?" She had a sudden thought. "Is it from Catherine?"

"How did you know?"

"I didn't. I just guessed. You are good friends, aren't you?"

"She's my best friend."

"What does she say in her letter? Is she coming back?"

"No." Florence had a very perplexed expression.

"Did she say why not?"

"Yes, she did. It's not her fault. She wants to come back. It's the family."

"But I thought that, since the mother died, they were getting their lives back together again."

"Yes, but her dad is taking control. Her mother was quite happy for her to study in seminary, but her dad never liked the idea. Neither did her grandmother."

"Yes, grandmothers have quite a lot of authority here in Taiwan."

"They want her to get married."

This was a sudden blow. There had been no hint of such an outcome. "How far has this gone?"

"There is a man called Chang. He works as a carpenter in the village. It has been arranged that she will marry him."

"How long has this been going on?"

"Not long, I think. Her dad arranged it with his dad."

"How well does she know him?"

"I don't think she knows him at all. She may have walked past him in the street. That is all."

"It seems so cruel."

"That is the way thing are done in Chinese society."

"But there are changes everywhere. It doesn't have to be like this."

"Yes, there are changes in the towns and cities; but in the countryside everything is still the same. It is her duty to her father to accept what he has arranged."

"Is there no way out?"

"If her father pulled out of it, he would lose face. Once the agreement has been made, that is it. The other family will hold him to it."

"And there is no consideration for what Catherine wants?"

"That is our tradition. Things are changing, but in the countryside it is still like that in many places. People learn to love each other in time."

Rose sighed. She felt as if she was up against a brick wall. Here was a girl who loved the Lord and wanted to serve him, and who had been studying with that aim in mind, and all this was to be ignored in the interest of securing a husband whom she did not even know. "I thank you for sharing that with me," she responded. "As you can see, I am very disappointed and I only wish there was something I could do."

"I wish that too, but there is nothing."

34

It must have been very frustrating for little Sandy. Here he was all geared up for a good walk, and his mistress kept stopping to talk with other human beings. They had just got out of the door and into the courtyard when it began.

The principal, Timothy Lee, carrying a big pile of books, was on his way to a lecture. Alleyne could see that this was no time for a long conversation, but she did not like to miss this opportunity. "Dr. Lee," she said, "has any decision been reached about my job?"

By the startled response, it was obvious that he had not even noticed her. "Very soon, very soon," he answered. "We will talk about it in a few days' time." With these words he moved on.

The not knowing was even worse than being told she had lost her job. She had communicated this uncertainty about the future to the mission and they had told her they would not consider any alternative until it was definitely established that she must leave her job. This only served to increase her sense of insecurity. It was most unkind of Dr. Lee to keep her waiting so long. The only advantage of such a delay was that it could be a hint that her job might be retained.

As she was reflecting on this, a figure came out of the library and only just missed standing on Sandy's tail. She stooped down to stroke him as if to make up for this threat. "That was a close thing," Rose said, looking up at her.

"I think he's forgiven you," Alleyne responded. "Everyone seems to be in such a hurry this morning."

"I just had some disturbing news ," Rose said as she straightened her body upwards.

"And what was that?" Alleyne was not ready for more disturbing news.

"It's about Catherine."

"Has she gone absent again? I haven't seen her yet."

"It's more serious than that. You know that her mother died?"

"Of course. It has been a sad time for the poor girl."

"Well, her father has taken matters into his own hands, and he has arranged a marriage for her."

"Presumably with a non-Christian whom she does not know"

"I'm afraid so."

"That used to happen a lot. Times are changing now, but it still happens in rural settings."

"Do you think there is anything we can do about it?"

"If the marriage is already arranged, it would be virtually impossible for her father to pull out of such an agreement." Sandy was beginning to show his impatience.

"Couldn't we go and reason with him?"

"And what good would that do? If the deed is already done, we are powerless to change anything."

"But it seems so unfair. She was enjoying her studies here, and she could have put them to good use."

"No doubt. I regret this just as much as you do, but there is nothing we can do to change the situation. I know, Rose, you can be quite persuasive, but in this instance there is nothing to be done, believe me."

Sandy whined in annoyance. This conversation was taking far too long. Humans could be so inconsiderate at times.

"I think Sandy is getting impatient," Alleyne admitted. "Like you, I would do anything to change the situation, but I think we just have to accept it. When you get into Chinese culture, you just have to take note that these things happen." With this, she began to walk on.

35

Peter almost collided with Miss Zimmer as he went to collect

Cynthia that morning. She seemed to be upset about something. Just as he was about to knock at the door of the guest room, Rose came up behind him. "I thought I saw you," she said.

"Is Cynthia awake?" he asked her.

"I don't think she slept very well. You never know how jet lag is going to affect you."

"Has she eaten any breakfast?"

"I brought her something, but I don't know whether she has eaten it. Let me go and see if she is respectable." She tapped at the door and called, and there was an answering voice from within. "Peter's here. Shall I tell him to come in?"

Cynthia answered this question by appearing at the door herself. "You see, I'm ready for you," she smiled as she admitted him. But her eyes were puffy, and he could see that she was struggling a bit.

Rose left them to themselves. Cynthia waved him to a chair whilst herself sitting on the bed. "I felt a bit warm in the night."

"That's nothing to what it will be like in the summer. We think of this as the cool season."

"Then it's a good job I didn't come in the summer, isn't it? This is quite warm enough for me."

This really was a test case. If Cynthia found she was able to cope with local conditions, then the possibility of marriage was opened to them again. Even so, they would have to be certain that there was enough love between them to make the relationship work.

"How do you feel about going over with me to the hostel and meeting some of the students? You could eat lunch with us all as well. Old Su is prepared for that."

"As long as they don't mind having a bleary eyed female in their midst."

"They all know what jet lag is," he reassured her, "even if most of them haven't experienced it. So they will make allowances."

"OK. Then I think I'm ready to go when you are. Just a moment." She ran a comb through her hair. "There, I think I'm as respectable as I'm going to be."

It was only a five minute walk from the seminary to the student hostel. As they walked down the alley, an old man on a bicycle suddenly came round a corner and just missed colliding with them.

"That was a near thing," Cynthia said.

"You get used to it. It is just a part of life here."

As they came to the outside gate of the hostel, a couple was just coming out. Paul was wheeling his moped, and Jenny was preparing to mount.

"So this is your girl friend," said Paul in his best English. "I'm pleased to meet you." He extended a hand to shake Cynthia's but withdrew it quickly to steady the machine.

"You're much braver than I am," Cynthia said to Jenny. "I'm so glad that Peter doesn't ride a motor bike."

"Pleased to meet you," Jenny said. It was not clear whether or not she had understood Cynthia's words. The two of them went roaring off down the road, and Peter and Cynthia walked down the track which led to the two buildings – Peter's home and the hostel itself.

They climbed the three steps and Peter opened the door to admit her.

"Is it all wooden floors like this?"

"Yes, it is a Japanese style house, and they are usually like this."

"I suppose that makes it cooler in the summer."

"That and the sliding doors, yes. I usually ask people to take their shoes off when they come in."

"I don't see any problem with that." They both slipped out of their shoes.

"This is my study," Peter told her. "I also hold English classes here sometimes."

"I didn't know that was part of the job."

"It is what people expect of you if you are a foreigner."

He took her round some of the other rooms, which were not currently in use, a guest room and the room that houses the worship. "It looks quite spacious," was her comment.
"And this is my living room," he commented. It was a small back room with space only for two chairs, a cupboard and some shelving.

"It looks very small," she said. "The study was much bigger."

"But this is for private use. Other people don't need to come here."

"What about the kitchen?"

"Back here." He took her to what was the last room in the building. It was a narrow room, and the door led out into a yard.

Cynthia looked disappointed. "There isn't much space," she complained. There aren't enough cupboards or working surfaces."

"I know it isn't ideal, but it's actually much better than some of the kitchens I have seen."

Just then a bell rang. Cynthia looked startled. "That's OK. It just means that lunch is ready. You will be able to meet some of the students."

"Do they know I can't speak their language?" Cynthia asked.

"Of course. They will be happy enough practising their English."

When they reached the dining room in the other building, only two of the tables were in operation. As this was Saturday, some of the students had other plans. They sat down together, and Mark thrust a bowl of rice before them.

"I'm not very good with chopsticks," Cynthia admitted.

"I think you are good enough to impress them," Peter said.

"Very pleased to meet you," Mark welcomed her. "Fu Mushr has told us a lot about you." ("My Chinese name", Peter whispered.)

"You sound American," Cynthia commented. Mark looked puzzled.

"When you have American teachers," Peter explained, "you tend to pick up the accent."

"We are very glad to see you at last." Wang Ming declared. "Fu Mushr is lonely. He needs a woman. Welcome to come to live here."

This seemed to embarrass Cynthia. Peter explained. "She is just here as a friend. We have not made any decisions about the future."

"You make a good wife," Wang Ming added, as if the matter was settled.

Somewhat belatedly, Peter introduced the two students who had spoken; then he introduced her to another student. "This is Simon. He only joined us last term. Unfortunately one of our students could not make the grade and he had to leave. Simon came to fill his place."

"It was very kind of Mr. Falconer to make room for me," Simon asserted. "I am very happy here. Here too I can learn more about the Christian faith."

"This is a good place to learn," said Joshua. Some of us are already Christians."

"I'm glad to hear it," said Cynthia. She seemed more at ease now among these students than she had been at the beginning.

After the meal they returned to the other house and drank tea together in the living room.

"Could you imagine ever living here?" Peter inquired.

"It would take some getting used to," Cynthia admitted. "It is so different from life back home. In any case, I've only just arrived, I'm feeling jet lagged, and it is hard to think straight."

"I must admit you've coped so far a lot better than I thought you would," Peter said.

"So you didn't have high hopes of me?"

"Sorry, I didn't mean to sound negative. But I remember when I first said I was coming out here you did all you could to dissuade me."

"Yes, I admit that. It was such a shock, I suppose I was overreacting."

"But it is not just about your ability to adapt, is it?"

There was a short silence. Cynthia stared into his eyes. "You're right. It's about us."

"I know we were much in love at the beginning. Sometimes I still feel that way. At other times I feel we have grown apart."

"That was my fault. I was dead against sharing your life out here."

"And now?"

"I could get used to it – if I felt that our love was real."

"Then that's what it boils down to, isn't it? Is our love strong enough to last?"

"Yes, I was aware of that question even before I set out. I knew that I still had a lingering love for you, Peter. That is why I wanted to keep in touch. Seeing you here again has brought back some of the old feeling. But is it true love?"

"That's what we need to find out."

"Has there been anyone else?" she asked him.

"Not really. A few casual friendships. Nothing serious. I suppose I've been too busy learning the language and everything."

"Yes, that must have taken up a lot of your time."

"And it has to be mutual. We must both feel the same. Anything short of real love and deep commitment to one another is not enough. And there is another thing. You must feel a real sense of call to this life. If it were just my own call, and you were living here just because of our relationship and nothing more, that could make life difficult for us both."

"Why must it get so complicated?"

"There is another complication. My mission would need to vet you. If we were getting married and they did not like you, we could both be out on our ear."

"Really?" She looked crestfallen.

"But don't worry. They are very caring. It's great to have you here."

Wordlessly, they embraced and kissed. Peter felt a surge of the old love coming back. He could imagine them both living together in this house and being like parents to the students. It was an attractive thought. The next few days would be crucial.

36

It was hard for Arnold to concentrate on the shop work that Saturday morning. Kathleen had telephoned from the hospital earlier to let him know that Sammy had had a good night. She had called some time later to tell him that the doctor had not been round yet, but that she thought he would agree to let Sammy come home. How much more convenient it would be if they each had a personal telephone that they could carry round with them. Maybe one day this would become commonplace.

At last the long awaited call came.

"It's ok," Kathleen told him. "Sammy's head is sore but there don't seem to be any long term ill effects. The doctor kept us waiting all morning but he just came round and said Sammy could go home. It's such a relief. I'm afraid I did not sleep very well for worrying about it."

"I'll come right over with a taxi."

"What about Philip?"

"He's at a friend's house. I'll just come alone."

"I can't wait to get him home again. It seems a lot longer than one night. Oh, when you come, bring his thick blue coat. I don't want him to get a chill."

"Will do."

When he got to the hospital, mother and child were both ready for the trip home. He looked around. So many of the other children were on drips. Kathleen sensed his thoughts. "They wanted to do that with Sammy too, but I wouldn't let them."

"It's criminal, sure it is. These kids have enough to be scared about without having that as well."

He had asked the taxi to wait so that there would be no delay in getting home.

Sammy was delighted to be leaving the hospital. He was as lively as ever, despite the sore head, and Arnold was relieved that things had been no worse. The taxi deposited then back home, and Kathleen prepared a cup of tea. Lunch could wait until they had collected Philip.

While Sammy played happily with his toys, the two of them, talked.

"I was so worried," Kathleen admitted. "It was so easily done. Those open drains are a menace. They should cover them up."

"It could've been a lot worse," Arnold said. "Let's be thankful for that."

"But it will never be quite the same when we are out together. I will be afraid of letting go his hand."

"Just because it happened once, it doesn't have to happen again. And I'm sure Sammy will be much more careful; in future. In any case, it isn't like being at home, where we could be blown up by a bomb at any time."

"Your home, not mine. But don't say things like that. At least, if anything happened there we would have family all around us. Here it feels a bit isolated."

"Let's face it. Nowhere in the world is perfectly safe."

"I don't find that reassuring. I want to live in a safe world, where I don't have to live with any fears."

"You know me. I'm happy to live in a dangerous world: I enjoy a challenge now and again."

"You can't really mean that."

"Sometimes life is too safe and too predictable."

"Well, I like it that way."

They were not going to agree about that.

37

Rose gave breakfast to Cynthia in her own room that Sunday morning. Although the room was small, there was enough room for them to balance trays on their knees as they ate and talked.

"How are you finding life in Taiwan?" Rose asked.

"Actually, it's easier living here than I thought it would be. I know there are lots of thing I am not familiar with – people brushing their teeth in the street and spitting into the gutter, bicycles and motor bikes that seem to come at you from all angles, a few smells that I'm not used to, things like that. But I'm getting used to it. It is easier to adapt than I thought it would be."

"Yes, you never know about that until you come to experience it for yourself." She wanted to ask how their relationship was progressing, but did not deem it wise to broach the subject. In a way, she would be happy to see them living and working together, even though it would mean she would never have a relationship with Peter herself. She could honestly say that she wanted the best for both of them.

"I hope you don't mind the cereal," she went on. "It was the best the rice puffer man could do. It isn't easy to get breakfast cereals in the shops here."

"I quite like it. We could do with a rice puffer man at home."

"When I go home," Rose remarked, "I'm spoilt for choice. There are so many goods in the shops that we can't buy here."

"Yes, I suppose we take a lot for granted."

"One piece of toast or two?"

"One is enough. At least you are not short of good bread."

"No, we have bakeries everywhere. Some of it, though, does

not taste like the bread at home; but you get used to it."

"I suppose I would've a lot to get used to if I came to live out here."

"It's surprising how you adapt. You soon feel like a native. When you have a sense of call, it makes it easier somehow."

"Yes, I suppose that's one thing I have to be sure about if our relationship goes any further. Do I have a sense of call? I know it isn't like moving into another job at home. If you come out here, you have to be sure that God has called you. Right now, I'm not sure about that. It was always Peter's call, not mine."

"If God really wants you here, he will call you as well."

"I am wondering how he will do it. It would be so much easier if you could hear an audible voice; but I know that God does not normally do it that way."

"He will make it clear one way or another. Yes, I agree that you need to be called independently from Peter."

"One reason for coming out here is to explore that a bit more. It is useful to see what sort of life I might be called to."

"Yes, it is much easier when you have tested the waters here to sense whether you have a call. Though, having said that, I got a call to missionary work, but did not know where I would end up. It could have been anywhere."

"That was brave of you to step into the dark."

"God knew what he was doing. It is not really the dark if he is in charge. I feel I am in the right place, and that is what matters most."

When breakfast was over, the two of them were to go to the church at St. John's. Normally Rose would attend the local Presbyterian church, but on this occasion she had decided to worship with the small English congregation and so keep Cynthia company.

As they stepped out, they noticed that there was a cold wind. Cynthia shuddered. "I didn't expect to find it as cold as this."

"This is the exception," Rose told here. If it gets cold in the winter, you know it will only be for a short time. It isn't like winter back at home."

They arrived in good time. Rose recognised Bill and Jenny from the seminary, and they greeted her warmly.

Peter told her he was pleased to see her, then disappeared again in order to get ready. Two of his students came in to join the congregation, and they were followed in by two American families. A couple with two children sat next to her. The mother said, "We are Tom and Vickie, and you're coming to eat with us afterwards."

"Yes, Peter said something about it. I shall look forward to it."

"It will be your introduction to American food," Vickie went on, smiling sweetly. "And who is this?"

Rose saw that some explanation was called for. "Cynthia is staying at the guest room in the seminary and I am looking after her."

"That is kind of you. So Peter has two lady friends."

Rose did not know what to make of this, so she stayed silent.

Vickie went on: "I don't think I have seen you before."

"No, I usually worship at the local Presbyterian church."

"In Chinese?"

"Yes. Taiwanese actually."

"That's very clever of you."

"I don't understand every word."

"I wouldn't understand even one word."

Peter came in wearing his robes. Rose had not seen him like this before. It was almost like looking at another person. For Cynthia it was different: this was how she must remember him from the church in Manchester. At least, this time Rose would be able to understand every word that was spoken.

38

At last Alleyne had persuaded her friend to join her at the local Presbyterian Church. Helen had complained that she would not be able to understand much of what was said, but Alleyne has reassured her that she would translate for her. "It is a good church," she explained, "and we enjoy very good expositions of scripture."

"I'll give it a try," Helen had agreed, "but I won't go there regularly. As you know, I have informal worship in English with a few friends, mainly those connected with my school, and I am well satisfied with that."

Although it seemed as if it was going to be a one-off, Alleyne was still glad to have the opportunity of introducing her friend to a church which meant so much to her personally. As she prepared to leave the house, Sandy wagged his tail.

"No, Sandy," she exclaimed, "you know this is Sunday morning I am going to church and they don't allow dogs there."

One last wag of the tail, and Sandy retired, defeated, to the comfort of his basket. These humans were not very good at recognizing their priorities.

Wearing her favourite hat, a blue one, Alleyne left the apartment and began to walk to the church. It was only five minutes away. Helen would have a much longer journey, but the buses were frequent, even on Sundays, so she ought to be able to arrive on time. A few of the seminary students were also coming out of their rooms in order to worship there. Although the seminary had its own chapel, students were encouraged to worship at other churches on Sundays.

Out on the street, life was bustling as if it were any other day of the week. One thing she appreciated about furlough was that the world of work on a Sunday for the most part shut down. Here it was a day like any other. A motor bike went past piled high with boxes which, in a Western country, would have needed a large van for delivery.

When she arrived at the church, folk were streaming in. She nodded to people whom she recognized and they nodded back. One lady invited her to go in with her so that they could sit together, but Alleyne explained that she was waiting for a friend.

As she stood there, she found her mind wandering. Once again she thought of her uncertain future. It was to be hoped some definite decision would be made soon about whether she was still required at the seminary so that, if some alternative should be needed, her mission would be able to act upon it. She liked a life that was clear and predictable: living with uncertainty was not something which came naturally to her.

She looked at her watch. Just two minutes to go. What had happened to Helen? She was usually a good timekeeper. Had she decided not to come? Had there been trouble with the buses? There were various possible explanations. She would wait till the last possible moment and then go in and sit at the back so that she could see Helen coming in.

It was time. The first hymn was just beginning, so she went in. It was hard to concentrate on the words of the hymn when her mind was still occupied with Helen's absence. Hopefully there would be a good explanation for this.

39

After the service, Peter and Cynthia were taken by the Eastwickers to their home near the base, some two miles away. Peter had been there before, but for Cynthia this would be a new experience. "Here in Taiwan," he had told her, "you have to adapt to two cultures – Chinese and American. They are both very different."

Their house was a large white wooden structure, with a well tended garden. As if reading Peter's thoughts, Vickie said: "I'm the one who looks after the garden. Tom always has other things to do."

"Now, honey, you know that's not true," Tom objected. "Didn't I mow the lawn last week?"

"All right, honey. I accept that."

They all spilled out of the car and Craig and Amy raced each other to the front door.

"I wish I still had all that energy," Vickie sighed.

"Now, honey," her husband interjected.. "You're not over the hill yet. You're a young woman in the prime of life."

Tom turned the key in the lock, and they all trooped indoors. There was a large living room, which must have taken up about half of the floor space. Behind this was a corridor, off which bathrooms and bedrooms and kitchen could be accessed. It was a bungalow, so it took up a big piece of ground. To people like the Eastwickers, it must have been just as if they had never left their own country.

"This is really nice," Cynthia exclaimed.

He could see why she liked it. This place was so Western that it was hard to believe you were in Taiwan. The large armchairs and sofas spoke of comfort and leisure, the paintings on the wall added a splash of colour, and there were even soft carpets beneath one's feet. It was as if the whole household had been transported in an instant from the USA.

"Now you just sit down and I'll bring you something to drink," Vickie said; and a few moments later she reappeared with glasses of Koolade. "The dinner should be ready very soon," she smiled.

"Vickie is always well organized," Tom exclaimed.

"It looks very homely," Cynthia suggested.

This met with negative stares. (Peter explained in a whisper: "They think you said 'homey' and that is not very flattering.)

Quarter of an hour later they were all sitting round the table at one end of the room. From there they had a good view of lawn, trees and flowers. A ray of sun shone in through the window and glinted on the glassware.

"I can draw the blinds," Vickie suggested, fearing that it was blinding Cynthia.

"No," she said, "I don't mind it. I like warm sunshine."

"My wife is always very thoughtful about the needs of others," Tom said, "but I think she overdoes it sometimes."

The meal was one of steak and vegetables with a side salad. "Help yourself to vegetables," Vickie said. They did so. Only Craig refrained.

"What about the vegetables?" his father asked.

"Don't like them."

"You'll have them like the rest of us. They are good for you." With these words, Tom scooped up a large helping of vegetables and slapped them down on his son's plate.

"Craig is just going through an awkward stage," Vickie whispered.

"I always eat my vegetables," Amy smiled, putting on a goody-goody expression.

"Yes," her father commented, "you are always a good girl. Craig frowned at this.

"Have you eaten in an American home before?" Vickie asked

Cynthia.

"No, I don't think I have. I don't know any other Americans."

"Don't think of us as typical," Tom said. "Americans come in all shapes and sizes and flavours."

"I wouldn't know what was typical," Cynthia replied.
"You'll soon learn."

"I had a cousin who lived in America, and he came on a visit," Cynthia said. "I'm not sure whether that counts."

"Half counts," Tom laughed. "You must go over on a trip some time."

"This Taiwan trip is enough for me right now."

Peter was pleased that she was making herself at home here. She had adjusted to Taiwanese culture well, but American culture was nearer to what she was used to. They were coming to the end of the main course. Craig put down his fork when there were still carrots on his plate.

"You haven't eaten your carrots," his father snapped.

"I think he has done very well," Cynthia interjected. Craig seemed encouraged by her response.

"Are you going to eat them?" Tom asked.

"No." Craig folded his arms.

"Then you had better go to your room. Now!"

Sullenly, the boy slunk away from the table and out of the room, leaving a stunned silence.

"That boy has to be taught some manners," Tom exclaimed.

Peter did not agree with this treatment, and he could tell that Cynthia didn't, but it seemed politic to remain quiet. After all, they had no experience of bringing up children.

The conversation from then on was rather more subdued. Amy, taking advantage of the situation, became very bubbly, and made the most of her popularity. Peter could see that there was a lot of sibling rivalry.

After the meal they spent a long time sipping coffee and talking. Tom was quite eloquent about Seattle and its greenery. "You must come over some time when we are back home," he suggested.

Peter thought it unlikely, but he agreed to the suggestion.

When it was time to leave, Tom drove them back to St. John's. As they alighted, and Tom drove away again, Cynthia remarked, "I can't help thinking of the way he treated that poor boy."

40

As usual it was a rush to get the children ready for bed before the meeting began. Kathleen had suggested that, in view of the traumas they had been through, they should cancel this week's meeting, but Arnold told her that he was very reluctant to do that. After all, Sammy seemed fine now. What possible excuse could they give for cancelling? Besides, he always derived benefit from this time of fellowship and sensed that the others did too.

So here they were bathing their sons and getting them ready for bed. The ritual was over, including a story and some prayer. The bell would be ringing at any moment.

"Mummy, can you stay with me?" Sammy asked.

"If he needs you, go ahead," Arnold assured her.

"Thanks. I think it is important."

The bell rang. "I'll answer it."

"Oh, Arnold. I don't think I will join the meeting tonight."

"Just as you feel, my dear." He was disappointed, but he could see that she was looking very fragile.

The first visitor was Sister Cecilia. "Am I the first?" she asked. "I must have cycled quickly."

"You are very welcome," Arnold assured her. "Kathleen's rather tired, so she won't be joining us tonight."

"Oh, I'm sorry to hear that. Is she not well?"

"She is ok, but needs a bit more sleep."

"Yes, we are all like that sometimes."

The next to arrive was Big Lil. She appeared, larger than life with a beam on her face. "It's all beginning tomorrow," she boomed.

"You mean the evangelistic meetings? Yes, I shall be taking some books with me to sell."

"They say that Paul Fennigan is a great preacher. God can use him mightily. I am praying that many souls will be won for Christ this week. We have been praying a lot for this in our little church."

Just then Tim came. "Sorry to be a bit late," he confessed.

"You're not late," Arnold assured him.

"I just met a friend and he gave me some news."

"Let me bring the coffee in and then you can share it – if it is that kind of news, that is."

While Arnold was in the kitchen, the bell rang again. Tim answered the door in Arnold's stead. It was Peter and Rose, and with them was a woman he did not recognize."This is my friend Cynthia over from England," Peter explained.

"That was an experience," Cynthia puffed. "I don't cycle much at home, but here it is quite an adventure."

They all shook her by the hand and welcomed her, and they were all seated when Arnold brought in some coffee and biscuits.

"It's been quite a hectic Sunday," Cynthia confessed, "but Peter said I would enjoy this meeting, so here I am. Not sure I could keep up this pace all the time."

"Turning to Tim, Arnold said,. "You told us you picked up some news."

"Yes, it is terrible news. I couldn't believe it when I heard it."

"What is it then?"

"It's about a woman called Helen Binch. She's a teacher at a girls' school."

"I know her," Rose responded. "She is Miss Zimmer's friend. Has something happened to her?"

"'Fraid so," Tim replied. "Seems like she was found murdered." Horrified gasps greeted this announcement. "She was stabbed. Probably happened last night, but she was not discovered until this afternoon. I don't have the details, but it must be true. The guy who told me is usually reliable."

"But that's terrible news," Rose said. "Does Miss Zimmer know?"

"It depends who she's met. Not a lot of people know yet. It's just that a friend of mine knows someone who works at the school."

"This is something we can pray about," Arnold said. "Do they know who did it?"

"Not yet. Early days yet. It happened at her home. Either someone broke in or it was someone she trusted."

"That poor woman," Big Lil interjected. "Alleyne Zimmer, I mean. She didn't make friends so easily. This will have shattered her."

"If she knows about it," Rose said.

"If she doesn't know," Sister Cecilia said, "then someone ought to tell her."

"And I suppose that someone is me," Rose admitted.

"That won't be easy," Peter exclaimed. "If you want someone with you ---"

" I can handle it," Rose said, "but I will need your prayers. Are we sure this is the truth and not just hearsay?"

"It's the truth all right," Tim stated. "I wish it wasn't, but it is."

Of all the company, it was Cynthia who looked the most shaken. When she saw that others were looking at her, she said, "I didn't think this sort of thing happened among missionaries."

"It doesn't," Peter assured her. At least, I have never heard of this sort of thing happening before."

"I suggest we still drink our tea and coffee," Arnold suggested. "Later on we can pray about this, and we can pray that Rose may know how to speak with Miss Zimmer when they meet."

This news cast a shadow over the whole meeting. Praise on this occasion was somewhat restricted, and the intercessions centred on this tragic event. Arnold had hoped that Cynthia, on this first visit, would enjoy the fellowship that this group provided, but it was obvious that she had been badly hit by the news.

41

It was hard for Rose to concentrate during the meeting. All she could think of was the terrible news that Tim had brought. How was she going to break this to Alleyne Zimmer? There was no easy way to do it. The poor woman had only one good friend, and that same friend had now been cruelly murdered. She found herself, instead of concentrating on the prayers, trying to work out how she could break the news sympathetically. There was all the uncertainty too of how Miss Zimmer would take it. In fact, it was impossible to predict how she would react.

The meeting concluded. As they were preparing to leave, Arnold came up for a quick word. "I'm sorry to bother you with this," he said. "I know you've already got a problem giving this news to Miss Zimmer, but there is also that other matter I mentioned to you. I need someone to go out with me into the villages with the book van. There would be a small wage, of course. If you can think of someone, preferably a young man, I would be very grateful. It needs to be someone who is good with people and has a real heart for the Gospel."

Rose knew the girls in the seminary well, but she did not have a lot of contact with the boys. She had asked the girls for help, and they had given her one or two names: now it was time to act upon this. "I will do what I can," she promised.

"I like to go out on Wednesdays if that is convenient."

"I'll do my best."

As they mounted their bicycles to start the return journey, Cynthia exclaimed: "I'm saddle sore already."

"Don't worry," Peter assured her. "It isn't a long trip."

Cynthia began with a wobble, but soon corrected herself.

"The offer's still there," Peter said, "if you would like me to go with you to Miss Zimmer's."

"No, I think it might upset her. She doesn't know you very well, but she knows me."

"If you'd like me to be there---" Cynthia began.

"No, she doesn't know you at all. I appreciate the offer, but I don't think it would work."

As they cycled on, Rose thought that Cynthia looked a bit more apprehensive than she had done on the way out. Maybe she thought the murderer was lurking somewhere near ready to continue his work. At the seminary gate, Peter took his leave, and the two ladies pushed their bikes through the gateway, watched by old Tan, and on to the area of the guest room.

"You are welcome to come to my place for a bit,"she offered.

"No, that won't be necessary. I'm rather tired, and I would just like to rest."

"Very well. And don't worry about the murder. This sort of thing has never happened before. It is a one-off. In any case, she lived in a rather remote area. It would be a brave man who would come into a busy seminary to commit a murder. Sleep well."

"Thanks for everything," Cynthia replied.

"I'll take the bicycle back to its owner."

"Thanks. I was wondering what to do with it."

Rose did this first. Her own bicycle she placed in the usual store room and locked it. Now there was nothing to stop her going to see Miss Zimmer.

Timidly she knocked on the door. This caused the dog to bark. There was no other immediate response. Perhaps Miss Zimmer was not at home. Just when she was about to turn away, the door opened.

Miss Zimmer looked surprised. "Why, Rose, what brings you here at this time of the night? Is your meeting over?"

"Yes, I just got back. When I was there I got some terrible news. I wasn't sure whether you had heard."

"I think I know what you mean," she said, tight-lipped.

"I want you to know I'm so dreadfully sorry."

"I don't want to talk about it. Now, if you'll forgive me." The door closed.

Rose stood there for a moment. It was impossible to know what was going on behind the mask. If it had been her own best friend, she would be flooding with tears; but Miss Zimmer was unpredictable. Was she grieving inside? Or did she genuinely feel no emotion?

As she was walking back, she met a student called Mary, who was walking in the opposite direction.

"Ah," said Rose. "Just the person I wanted to meet. We were talking the other day about finding someone to go with the book van. You gave me two names."

"Did I?" Mary pondered for a few moments. "Oh yes, Martin and Frank."

"I need to see one or both of them. Maybe in chapel tomorrow."

"Martin's got a part time job. It's the only way he can pay his fees. But I think Frank is still available."

"Does he know anything about it?"

"No, Li Lausu. You would have to ask him yourself. He is good with people. I think he would do a good job. And I know he needs a bit of extra money."

"I will talk to him then tomorrow. Thanks for that."

The next morning, Rose attended chapel as usual, and was surprised to notice that Miss Zimmer was absent. Perhaps it was hard for her to face people in the present circumstances. At the end of worship the principal had a lot of announcements to make. At last, with a flip of his gown, he dismissed the students and staff.

Rose knew Frank by sight, so she drew alongside him as they were leaving the chapel. "Frank," she said, "I just wanted to ask you something."

Frank seemed surprised. He looked at his watch. "I've a class in ten minutes."

"This won't take long. Can we talk?"

They walked and talked at the same time. Rose explained Arnold's need for an assistant, and asked Frank if this was something he might enjoy doing.

"It all depends," Frank answered.

"Depends on what?"

"On my classes. If it coincides with my classes, I don't think my teachers would be very happy about it."

"I expect Mr. Maguire would bear that in mind. It would not be a big salary, but it might just help you a little bit."

"Extra money is always welcome."

"And I gather you get on with people."

"They get on with me. I suppose it all amounts to the same thing really."

"So you think you might be interested?"

"I will think about it."

"If you think you would like to talk with Mr. Maguire, I could give you his telephone number, or you could see him at the shop."

"Yes, I may do that. Does he know much about me?"

"Not at present. He doesn't even know your name. So if you have any secrets, he doesn't know them."

"Secrets?" Frank looked a little alarmed.

"I'm sorry, "Rose went on. "I didn't mean that you had any."

"OK."

As she walked away, Rose wondered why Frank had seemed momentarily troubled. Did he really have secrets? Was he the wrong man for the job?

42

It was as if Sandy knew that something was wrong. He lay there on the rug in a subdued mood, and the tail was as stationary as a lamp post.

Alleyne sipped her coffee, her second of the morning. Normally she would not have indulged herself like this, but she felt that in these circumstances such behaviour was justified. People might be wondering why she had missed chapel, but that did not concern her. It was better to be absent from view than to break down emotionally when in company.

She had always believed that when God called a person to be a missionary he also bestowed on them all the qualities needed for the task. Looking back over her career, she reflected on the many emergencies which she had faced, and the almost miraculous way in which she had been able to handle each one of them. That was the sign of being a good missionary: you were in control of the situation because God was in control of you.

The tragedy had affected her much more deeply than she cared to admit. Helen was the one person whom she could regard as her friend, and she had been taken from her in the cruellest of ways. As she thought about this, she was close to tears, but to give in to her grief would be a sign of weakness. She had always prided herself in her strength, and, although it was now being tested, she would prevail.

In a way, poor Helen had asked for this. She had insisted on living in a remote part of the suburbs. She had employed a cook who had a sense of menace about him. Surely he must be the one who had done it. He had probably noticed how she kept a lot of money in the house and decided to help himself. The trouble with Helen was that she trusted people too much. She refused to see that the presence of such a man in her house could be regarded as dangerous. In a way she had brought this tragedy upon herself.

She had to admit that she and Helen were equally strong-willed. Maybe that was what had brought them together, for they admired this trait in one another. But the downside was that this had closed Helen's ears to any warnings that others might give. She had always been able to cope and she would cope still.

For Alleyne, all this came on top of her anxiety about the uncertain future. It was time that the principal told her once and for all whether she could hold on to her job. The sooner he told her, the sooner her society could make some decision about her redeployment. What she feared most was that they would give her some homeside job and thus take her away from the Chinese people whom she loved. For her the USA was a foreign country, simply to be endured for short periods when she was on furlough. The very idea of living there on a more permanent basis filled her with apprehension.

But, again, she did not like to tell others about her fears. God had a plan for her life. To doubt this would be a sign of great weakness. The last thing she wanted was for people to come up to her offering sympathy and understanding. She was steady enough in her own faith to handle any kind of emergency, whether it involved murder or redundancy. Had not she been able to handle that traumatic event of being driven out of the China she loved? Compared with that, everything else was minor.

Soon she would have to go and teach a class. For once in her life, she regarded the prospect with some foreboding. She would need strength to hide her emotions. The students must see her as the confident, controlled person that she always was. Anything less than that would be a sign of weakness.

She set down her coffee cup, and whispered a short prayer, asking God to uphold her, so that nobody would suspect that she was in any way upset.

As she got to her feet and collected together her lecture notes, Sandy did not even look up. It was as if he knew this was not time for a walk and that he must not interfere with his mistress's thoughts.

43

Simon had shown interest in the Christian faith ever since moving into the hostel. Every Wednesday evening there would be a meeting for the students, and on these occasions he would often ask searching questions. When he heard that there were to be evangelistic meetings in the town, he expressed great interest. So it was that, on the first evening, Peter arranged to go with him. Peter invited Cynthia to go as well, with the encouragement that the message would be in English, translated into Chinese, but she indicated that she would rather relax. So he left her in the living room of his home, reading a book.

The setting was Chung Cheng Road Presbyterian, as this was the largest church in town. Even though they arrived half an hour early, it looked as if it would be hard to find a seat. On the way in, Peter nodded to Arnold, who has set up a well stocked bookstall in the foyer, and there were already prospective customers leafing their way through the books.

They managed to find two seats near the front. Casting his eyes around, Peter noticed Joshua with a friend, presumably a non Christian whom he hoped to introduce to the Lord. There was one of his night school students with a woman whom he took to be his wife. Big Lil was there too with several of her Chinese friends. There was an air of expectancy.

The visiting speaker, Paul Fennigan, was a slight figure with a wispy moustache. When, the preliminary worship completed, he stood up to speak, he showed that he had a powerful voice which contrasted strongly with his appearance. The translator, who was a local minister, copied all the mannerisms of the American in an attempt to be faithful to the message.

The talk was all about Nicodemus and the need to be born again. Peter was, of course, very familiar with the story, but the speaker interpreted it in a very dramatic and forceful way, so that he commanded the full attention of all those present. At the end he made the expected appeal. Billy Graham could not have done it any better.

Immediately a stream of enquirers surged to the front, where a team of counsellors waited to assist them.

"I have to go," Simon declared. Peter smiled as he watched his student join the others at the front.

As there were so many enquirers, this process took a long time. When Simon came back he was glowing with happiness: it was obvious that something special had happened to him. The speaker took five more minutes to explain how the new converts should help themselves to grow in their new faith; after which the pastor of the church pronounced a benediction and they were free to go.

"I feel like a new person," Simon explained as they joined the throngs leaving the church. "I know I have the strength to face all my problems now."

"What will your parents think of this?" Peter asked.

"They won't understand," Simon replied. "They follow traditional religions. I won't tell them yet. When I think it is right, then I will tell them."

Peter knew that in the villages, people were very conservative, and they would perceive Christianity as a threat to their way of life. For this reason, he was not surprised at Simon's caution. Their bicycles were still where they had left them: they unlocked them and cycled back to the hostel.

"I will tell the others," Simon asserted as they came in through the gate. "I want everyone to know. This is the best day of my life."

Peter wondered whether Cynthia would still be in the house, or whether she would have gone back to her guest quarters. What greeted him was a surprise. Cynthia was not alone. Seated with her was young Craig.

"We have a visitor," Cynthia said. "This was stating the obvious." Craig was looking somewhat sheepish.

"What is all this about?" Peter asked. "Do your parents know you are here?"

"We had an argument," Craig said. "I couldn't dig it, so I came here."

"You ran away?" The boy nodded. "Why here?"

Cynthia offered her explanation. "Yesterday, when we were at their house, he could see he had a friend in me." Craig decided not to add to that, but cast his eyes downward.

"Do your parents know you are here?" Peter asked. The boy shook his head. "They must be worried stiff. It's getting on for 11 o'clock. "Cynthia, did you not think of telling them?"

"Craig trusted me. I didn't want to let him down."

"But there's no way we can avoid telling them. They would not sleep a wink for worry about him." He turned to Craig. "You do realize that, don't you?"

"They will be really mad at me," Craig confessed.

"I think they will be so relieved to get you back that they will be ready to forgive you."

"My Dad gets really angry at times," Craig confessed. "It isn't the first time I've wanted to run away."

"But you do see how impossible it is for us to let you stay?"

"I suppose so," the boy mumbled.

"Can you give me your home phone number?"

Reluctantly the boy gave it to him and he dialled the number. It was the mother who answered the phone. The relief which she showed at this explanation was palpable. "One of us will be over to fetch him."

"Could I suggest that you come yourself? I think Craig might find that a bit easier."

"I will have to discuss this with my husband. One of us will come. The other will have to stay with Amy."

While they waited, Peter sought to calm the boy's fears. "I know your parents really love you. Maybe your Dad is hard on you sometimes, but I expect he means well. We are here to be your friends, but we can't take the place of your parents. You do know that, don't you?"

The boy nodded without speaking.

When Vickie arrived, there were tears of relief on her cheeks. "I was so worried," she exclaimed as she embraced her son.

"I think he was afraid of his Dad," Peter ventured. "If you can do anything to calm him down---"

"He's not an easy man to live with. But I know he loves you, Craig, he really does." She gave him an extra hug as if trying to prove it.

When they had gone, Peter and Cynthia discussed the subject.

"Thanks for looking after him," Peter said.

"I didn't know what to do. I was waiting for you."

"But in the meantime you managed to comfort him. You would make a good mother." He tried to imagine what it would be like to raise a family with her.

"I think I had better be getting back," Cynthia suggested.

"Oh, we have a problem."

"What is that?"

"Old Tan locks the gate at 10. You could climb over the wall."

"I don't think I would be very good at that."

"Or you could stay in the guest room here overnight."

"That sounds like a much better idea."

"Good. Then that's decided."

"You seem to have such a busy life," Cynthia intimated as they made up a bed for her to use. "I don't know whether I could keep up with it all – looking after the students in the hostel, teaching those at the university, running the church services and dealing with the American community. It would leave me breathless."

"These would not be your responsibilities. If ever we should get together, you would be there to support me. I might need a shoulder to cry on now and again. You would also find a niche to use your own talents."

"I can't imagine you crying. You always seem so strong."

"Not as strong as you might imagine. Now I hope you will be comfortable here."

"I'm sure I shall. Thanks."

44

Arnold was well satisfied with his sales on the first evening of the evangelistic meetings. If every night were the same, the takings would contribute much to the viability of the shop.

Now it was the following morning, and he was waiting in the shop for the appearance of the student, Frank, to see whether he would be willing and able to assist him on the road trips. Miss Lee had just prepared a cup of tea for both of them when the door opened and a young man came in. He wore a white open-necked shirt, a green pullover and shabby grey trousers.

"Mr. Maguire?" the young man asked in English.

"Yes. You must be Frank."

"That's right."

"You are looking for someone to help you?"

"Yes, do come into the inner room and we will talk about it. Miss Lee, please prepare another cup of tea."

When they were seated, Arnold asked Frank if he would like to speak in English or Mandarin, and he chose to speak in English. Many young people in Taiwan liked to have opportunity to practise their English, as this was often a passport to success.

They began with small talk. "Do your parents come from Mainland China or are they local?"

"They are local. We speak Taiwanese at home. We only use Mandarin when we have to. It is not fair to try to make everyone speak Mandarin. We like to speak our own language."

"Yes, I can agree with you. I learned Mandarin because I was told to; but I have a lot of sympathy for you local Taiwanese."

"Not many foreigners take trouble to learn our language. They think Mandarin is enough. Li Lausu is not like that. She speaks Taiwanese very good."

"Very well. Yes, she does. She puts us all to shame."

"Are your parents paying your fees at the college?"

"Yes, but it is hard for them. They cannot pay enough. That is why I have to look for other work. If I do not find other work, I have to leave college."

"If you are able to help me on my trips, I could not afford to pay you a lot; but I hope it would be enough to help you."

"Every little helps. Is that what you say?"

"Yes, that's how we put it. I usually make these trips about once a fortnight. It would be a whole day event, usually on Wednesdays. How does that fit in with your classes?"

"I have to ask permission. If I explain to them, I think they give me free time. As long as I work hard after I get back."

"I most often go out on Wednesdays. Do you have many classes on that day?"

"Only two – and they are not important ones. I think they will let me help you; but I need to ask them."
"Let me tell you what it would involve. Obviously we are partly there to sell books. But it is also a matter of making contact with people. People come up out of curiosity, and we are able to talk with them about the Lord. I trust you have experience of doing that."

"A bit. I know I can learn more."

"It would be good practice for you."

"Yes. Out in the villages they would speak Taiwanese. I prefer that."

"I'm afraid my Taiwanese is virtually non-existent."

"A pity. When you speak Taiwanese you can understand people better. And they like you more."

"It would be hard to learn another language. It might upset my Mandarin."

"I don't think so. You should try it."

"If you are with me there will be no problem: you can speak to them."

"You will not understand what I am saying. How do you know I say the right things?"

"I think a lot of your teachers at the seminary speak

Taiwanese."

"Yes. That is good. Most of the students are Taiwanese."

"It would certainly be useful to have a Taiwanese speaker in the villages."

"Then you will give me the job?"

"Yes, I can try you out. See if the college can give you some time on Wednesdays."

"I will ask them and let you know."

They finished their coffee, and Frank set off back to his college.

45

Mid morning the next day, Rose was marking some English papers when there was a tap at the door. When she opened it, she was surprised to find Catherine standing there.

"Did you miss me?" the girl asked her in Taiwanese with a twitch of the eyebrow.

"We all did. We felt sorry for you in your situation"

"Yes, it has been very difficult."

On a sudden impulse, Rose said, "Shall we go out and get a fruit ice? My treat." After saying this, she hesitated. The cold weather was not the best time for sampling fruit ice. "Or maybe some coffee?"

"That would be good." Obviously, Catherine felt comfortable.

As they walked through the college grounds and out on to the street, Rose asked, "Is this just a short visit?"

"Yes. I have a day to spare and I wanted to see my friends."

"Then I am honoured that you should come to me."

"You were always so good to me."

Just a few yards down the road was the shop that sold fruit ice in the summer and hot drinks all the year round.

The place was a relic of times past. For most people, ice was easily obtained through the use of a refrigerator; here there was a process involving whirring machinery and conveyor belts which in the end produced crushed ice. Preparing coffee was not as dramatic. Many students enjoyed coffee, despite the expense, because it was regarded as modern and Western.

"Now do tell me more of your situation," Rose invited, as they began to drink.

"There is not much to tell. You know about my marriage?"

"Unfortunately, yes. Who is the bridegroom?"

"His name is Chang. He is a carpenter."

"How well do you know him?"

"I only met him once. I don't really know what he is like.

"So you have no idea what to expect."

"It is the old custom. Marriages always used to be arranged."

"It seems so unfair that you have to spend your whole life with someone you have not chosen."

"It often works out well. You'd be surprised. People know they have to get on well together, so they make the most of it."

"But it is hardly ideal, is it? I presume he is not a Christian. Have you got a date for the marriage?"

"Next month."

"That soon?"

"It is what my parents decided."

"And am I right in thinking he is not a Christian?"

"I don't know him yet."

"Where will you live?"

"There is a spare room at his family compound. We will live there."

"It does not sound very private."

"Here in Taiwan it is often like this."

"I know. How do you feel about the marriage?"

"I don't know. It is what my father wishes."

"Do you think you can love this man?"

"I don't know that either. I've said that I don't really know him."

"And there is no chance of resuming your studies?"

"No. I have to be a good wife."

"I am so sorry. You were doing so well."

"Sz Lausu did not think so."

"All that is past. You had a lot on your mind at the time."

Catherine screwed up her eyes. "I liked being a student. I learned a lot. It has been hard to give up."

"I know it has. I only wish we could welcome you back. Is there still no way you could pull out of this arrangement and come back to us?"

"If I did not go ahead with it, my father would lose face."

Rose understood the implication. In Chinese society losing face was regarded almost as a fate worse than death.

"Maybe this was God's will for me after all – that I should marry this man."

"You think then that you have peace about it?"

"I cannot struggle against it. It has been decided for me. All I can do is accept it."

As they rose from the table and began to walk back, Rose said, "I appreciate that you came to see me. You know that I will be here for you any time you wish to talk."

"Yes, I know that. I am very grateful to you."

"And now I suppose you would like to see your friends."

"Yes, if they have come out of class. I would like to see them very much."

"The Lord's will be done," Rose said as they separated; but in her heart she felt very angry that a young girl's life should be thrown away like this.

46

Alleyne was marking papers in her flat when the summons

came. Hearing the tap at the door, she shouted, "Come in!" The door opened, and in came a student who was not one of her pupils – a tall and gangly girl with an awkward manner. "The principal wants to see you."

So it had come at last. Now she would find out whether her services were still required. She set out with some trepidation, though she tried not to show it. Hadn't she always maintained that a missionary must always be in control of her emotions?

Dr. Lee's study door was closed. She knocked firmly and went in. To her surprise she found that the principal was not alone. With him was a man in a dark suit. "I was hoping that you would be available," Dr. Lee said. This is Inspector Nee from the police department. Don't worry, you have not done anything wrong. He just wants to talk with you. I have to go and teach, so you may use my office." With these words he collected up his books and left the room. Alleyne was left to deal with this situation without his support.

Her immediate reaction was one of disappointment. Although she was dreading the possibility of being told that there was no longer any work for her, at least it would be better than living with uncertainty. Then her mind turned to the current situation. Why did Inspector. Nee want to see her?

Inspector Nee stepped forward and shook her by the hand, obviously under the impression that this was the best way to deal with foreigners. "It was good of you to come," he said in halting English. Then he apologized, "My English is not good."

"We don't have to speak in English," Alleyne explained. "I speak Taiwanese."

"Not Mandarin?"

"No, I speak the language of the people. Are you Taiwanese?"

"Yes, but I speak Mandarin most of the time," he said in Taiwanese.

"Then we will speak in Taiwanese."

Neither of them would have felt comfortable sitting at the desk; so they found two other chairs and arranged them so that they were facing one another.

The inspector avoided the preamble that was usually expected in such conversations "I understand that you are a friend of Miss Binch."

Alleyne wanted to reply, "I was", but there was no way of using a past tense in Taiwanese; so she simply nodded agreement with the statement and added a 'yes'.

"You have heard of her murder?"

"Yes. I was very sorry to hear about it."

"I am trying to find out all I can about her last moments. When did you last see her?" He had taken out a pen, and now he was twisting it round with his fingers, removing and replacing the cap. Alleyne concluded that he had not been an inspector for long.

"When did you last see her?" he asked.
"Last Thursday. I went to her place for a meal. It was the first time."

"Did you notice anything unusual?"

"I said it was the first time. How was I supposed to know what was usual?"

"Maybe you can give me your impressions."

"I told her that it was a lonely place to live. I said she should move nearer to the town centre, but she wouldn't listen to me. She said she was very comfortable living there."

"As you say, it is a very quiet spot."

"She could be very stubborn," Alleyne went on, not realizing that she could be talking about herself.

"When you were there, did you get a good look at her cook, a Mr. Yu?"

"I saw him, but he was hard to get to know. He seemed like a very secretive person."

"Do you think he was the kind of person who could commit murder?"

"Now, how I am I suppose to answer that one? I would not

have employed him. I found it hard to trust him; but Helen was satisfied with him."

"You see, he has disappeared. He has a home just round the corner, but he is not there. Nobody has seen him since the murder."

"So he is the one you suspect?"

"Of course. There was no sign of a break-in. We could not find the knife that was used, but it was probably a normal kitchen knife such as he would use when preparing meals. Everything points to this being an inside job."

"I can see why you suspect him."

"Do you think he was the kind of person who would behave like this?"

"It does not really surprise me."

"Another thing – did your friend keep much money in the house?"

"Yes, that was because she did not trust the banks. I told her it was dangerous to leave so much money about but she would not listen. Was there still money about the house?"

"No. Just small change. It looks as if robbery was the motive."

"If only she had listened to me."

"This has been very helpful. It does rather sound as if our suspicions are confirmed. You would not know if he had friends or relatives in some other place? Some place he might have gone to?"

"I have no idea. It did not come into the conversation. Helen trusted him; but he kept to himself, and I doubt whether even she could have answered your question."

"That is OK. I did not really expect you to be able to tell me anything."

"Tell me, did she suffer?"

"Do you really want to know? She was stabbed several times. It must have been very painful. I doubt whether the first stab finished her off. There are signs that she fought back."

Alleyne felt tears coming into her eyes, and tried not to show it.

Standing up, the inspector said, "If you think of anything you have not told me, please come to the station."

"Of course I will."

"And it has been a pleasure to speak with someone who understands Taiwanese."

47

That evening, in a small restaurant, as they were just finishing a Chinese meal, Peter and Cynthia were engaged in conversation.

"I wonder," Cynthia reflected, "whether I matter to you or not."

Peter raised his eyebrows. "What makes you say that?"

"You've been so busy since I got here. We have had so little time together – and I came all this way."

"I know it's difficult, Cyn, but I still have my work to do. If you had come in a holiday period---"

"I told you it wasn't convenient."

"Well, I still have my work to do. As you can see, I have a busy teaching programme at the university."

"I know. And the students here need you; and then there's your Sunday congregation and any runaways they might have, not to speak of big meetings in town."

"Yes, this happens to be a busy period." A girl filled their glasses once more with hot water. By this time the tea was virtually tasteless.

"I suspect it is always a busy period with you. I'm not sure whether I could live like this."

"Whoever you marry, whether it is me or someone else, they will still have their regular work to do. A man has to earn his living."

"I know, but you seem to be busier than most."

"Well, you did come out here to test the waters, didn't you? To see whether you could fit into this kind of environment? To see whether our relationship could work out under these conditions?"

"Yes, I rather surprised myself. I didn't think I had it in me."

"All credit to you, Cyn, for doing that. And you have fitted in very well."

"But it's not just the work. I'm not sure I could handle the language -"

"You could have lessons."

"And the road conditions and the weather and the habits of local people and everything else."

"You soon learn to acclimatise."

"You might. I'm not sure about myself."

"It is hard to tell when you are only here for a few days. I think you have coped well up to now."

"And then I must say there are other things. That gruesome murder---"

"That is not typical. It was a one-off."

"It didn't do much to build up my confidence, that's all I can say. Now don't get me wrong. I'm glad I came. I really respect the work you're doing. But the big question is whether I could settle into this kind of life and be happy."

"That would depend on our relationship, wouldn't it?"

"Couldn't you take a bit more time off to be with me?"

"I already told you about tomorrow. I don't have any classes in the daytime, and I said we could go to Blue Lake."

"Yes, I must admit I am rather looking forward to that."

The next day dawned fine, and after breakfast they caught a bus to travel the 20 miles or so to the lake. Unfortunately the bus was so full that they had to stand. When they came to their destination, they had to walk down a slope to the lake's edge.

"I think it's going to be a hot day," Cynthia remarked, mopping her brow.

"Not really," Peter said. "You should see what it's like in the summer. Today it won't be any more than 72 degrees or so – cool by our standards."

"That would be a heat wave back home. How high does it get in the summer?"

"Mostly around 97."

"How can you survive? I would be roasted."

"You get used to it. And more places these days have air conditioning. In fact, sometimes it is so strong that you even feel cold."

"Well, today's quite hot enough for me."

They came to a place where boats were available for hire, and Peter made arrangements with the boatman, who was wearing a striped tee-shirt. Cynthia stepped gingerly into the boat and Peter took up the oars. As they began their journey, a gentle wind blew them on their way.

"I must admit that it's lovely round here," Cynthia remarked as she gazed around here. This is much better than living in a big town like yours."

"There are plenty of places like this," Peter assured her, "where you can come for relaxation."

"Now at last I am beginning to feel like a tourist."

Another boat passed them. It contained a party of young people: a transistor radio was blaring out pop music and they were beating time with their arms.

"You get that sometimes," Peter explained. "The young people love to imitate Westerners. A lot of them would love to go and live in the West."

"And make lots of money and enjoy a comfortable lifestyle? Yes, I can picture that. It must seem like a paradise."

"Well, you just concentrate, Cyn, on enjoying this other paradise. "

"Yes, it really is a beautiful place. I'm impressed."

"Do you want a turn at the oars?"

"No, I'm perfectly happy to let you do all the hard work," she said with a grin. They rounded a bend and a long but narrower section of the lake stretched before them.

They carried on for a while in silence. After a while Cynthia asked, "What's that tree over there?"

"It's a banyan tree."

"I'm impressed."

"You needn't be. We've got one in the yard at the hostel. That's how I know it."

"OK. I understand."

After a little while, Peter said, "We'd better turn round and head back again or we might be late delivering the boat back"

"I can just hear them bawling, 'Come in, number 7'."

Peter suited word to action; but he found it hard pulling the oars against the wind. "A bit harder this way," he complained.

"Yes, I can see that it is a bit of a struggle."

Talking was somewhat restricted for the next twenty minutes or so, as Peter needed all his energy for the rowing. Cynthia teased him a bit. At last they drew into the shore with about 3 minutes to spare.

They had brought picnic things with them, and found a pleasant spot under the shade of trees to share it. As they bit into their sandwiches they resumed the conversation.

"Well, we've had a few days together," Peter said. "How do we feel about each other?"

"You know," Cynthia began, "when we first met in Manchester I fell head over heels in love with you. I'm not ashamed to admit it. I never thought that sort of thing would happen to me. How did you feel about me?"

"I felt very fond of you at the time. But I didn't want to rush into anything – especially as I was not clear about the future."

"Only 'fond of'? Not 'love'?

"Sometimes it is hard to distinguish between the two."

"Did it blossom into love?"

"It got very close at times."

"I loved you until I heard you were going away. It felt like a kind of betrayal. All the hopes I had for our life together were shattered."

"It wasn't meant to be."

"I know. That's just how it felt at the time. Another sandwich?"

"Thanks. Yes, you know that my main aim, was to follow God's will – whatever the cost."

"Couldn't you have thought of it as God's will to stay at home?"

"That was not how it appeared to me."

"I know. That was when the relationship went wrong."

"It wasn't easy for me. Although we did not have a commitment, we were close to making one."

"I know." There were tears in her eyes. "Sometimes I wish... But it's no good harping on the past.

"I still have a lot of regard for you," Peter said.

"Yes, I felt that when you kissed me last night. But it has to be more than that, doesn't it?"

"Has coming here changed anything?"

"I think I might just possibly be able to get used to living here, but it would be a struggle."

"That is some progress. But that is not the main thing, is it?

Could we imagine being together for the rest of our lives?"

"If I really loved you, I think I could do it."

"And do you?"

"If I felt that you really loved me …."

"It's not the same, Cyn, as it was in the early days."

"I know, but I had to come here to find out for myself."

"We still have a few days to work on this."

Cynthia was silent for a moment; then she said, "What do you think of Rose?"

Peter felt a little embarrassed at the question.

"I can tell she is very fond of you," Cynthia went on.

"Is she? I never thought of it."

"Come on, you must have given it some thought."

"A bit, but I did not take it very seriously. I was thinking of <u>you</u>."

"If our relationship doesn't work out, do you think you will want to get to know her better?"

"I think we should concentrate on <u>our</u> relationship at the

moment. If this doesn't work out, then it will be time to think of other things. I'm going to try one of these Yakults."
"What's that?."

"It's a kind of yoghurt drink. Want one?"

"I don't think so."

They fell silent again. It looked as if they had no future together; but it was not yet a forgone conclusion.

48

The evening meal at the Maguire home was over. Arnold sat back, feeling relaxed. "That was a good meal, sure it was," he declared.

"Nice to be appreciated," Kathleen replied.

"I really meant it, sure I did."

"Can we leave the table?" Philip asked.

"Why don't we take a walk?" Arnold suggested. "Bedtime can wait for a bit." Philip greeted the suggestion with pleasure.

Kathleen, however, did not appear to be very enthusiastic. "I'm not sure whether it's a good idea."

"Why not?"

"The boys are tired. They need their sleep."

"No, we're not," Philip said. "Honest. Isn't that right, Sammy?" Sammy nodded agreement, for it had been said by his older and wiser brother.

"So we can go then," Arnold said.

"I don't think I feel like going," Kathleen objected.

"But it wouldn't be the same going without you."

"Maybe another time."

Arnold faced a dilemma. Should he listen to his wife and his sons? "I know," he said at last. "Let's have a game of football in the yard." This alternative suggestion met with approval from the boys and the matter, for the moment, was resolved. Arnold could not help wondering, however, why his wife had objected so strongly to his proposal.

When the boys were safely tucked up in bed , bedtime stories had been read and extra glasses of water produced, and the two of them were sipping their coffee together, Arnold brought up the subject.

"What was the real reason for not wanting to go out?" he asked.

Kathleen became tearful. "I'm sorry," she said.

"What is the problem? You can tell me."

"You will think I'm being overdramatic."

"Try me."

"It's just that Sammy's accident took a lot out of me."

"In what way, dear?"

"I keep seeing it happen. It could have been so much worse. It could have affected him for the rest of his life."

"But it didn't, did it? He's fine now. There's nothing wrong with him."

"But I'm scared of it happening again."

"It's not going to happen. That was a one off. In any case, it means we will be extra careful with him now."

"I know all that, but I can't help feeling as I do. I feel it is a big risk bringing up our two boys in this environment."

"But you've never felt like this before. I thought we were both agreed that this would be a big adventure for them. They both love it here."

"I know. But I can't help it. I just can't get that accident out of my mind."

"I told you, it's over and done with."

"Not in my mind, it isn't."

"You'll get over it in time."

"I'm not sure whether I will."

"But we can't mollycoddle them over this. We still have to go out and do things together."

"Arnold, don't expect me to be rational. Just try and understand how I feel at the moment."

"I'm trying. I'm sorry the whole incident has taken so much out of you. But your feelings will change."

"Will they? I'd like to think so. But I'm not sure. I never used to worry before: it's as if I've changed; and I'm afraid I can't change back"

"Let's give it time. It only happened a few days ago."

"I've been thinking. You're not entirely happy with the work, are you?"

"It has its moments; but, yes, I suppose I have to admit it gets a bit dull at times."

"You might be happier back at home doing journalism again."

"But we felt it was God's call to come here."

"It was. But it doesn't have to be a call for life."

"We both thought it was long term."

"God can call us out, but he can also call us back again."

"I would want to be sure it was really God calling and not just some idea of our own."

"Of course. We would have to be agreed."

"This is all to do with your fears about Sammy, isn't it?"

"Yes, I have to admit that."

"There was never any problem until now. And we entrusted our lives and the safety of our children to God, didn't we?"

"I know we did. God has been good to us. But I can't help feeling as I do."

"As I said, this should pass."

"But if it doesn't, can we think about the future? We go home on furlough this summer, as you know. It would be a good time to review our position."

"You've taken me completely by surprise. We both expected to come back here after furlough."

"But I think you have had doubts about the future as well. Am I right?"

"Well, yes, I have wondered. But I thought if the book work was not right we might find something else."

"You're a good journalist and I feel your talents are wasted here."

"Maybe so. You've taken me aback and I must say I find it hard to think straight right now."

"But we can give some serious thought to the future, can't we?"

"Of course. Whatever we do, it has to be something we've decided together, and we've got to both be sure it's the Lord's will."

"I know. That goes without saying."

"We both need time to think this out – and to pray, of course. I'm happy to stay on here if I'm sure it is the right thing to do."

"But there is Philip's education as well."

"That's true. We haven't really discussed that. We did talk a bit about home schooling, but we really have to talk a lot more about that."

"But you will promise me to give all this more thought?"

"Of course. And we must make sure we fully understand each other on this."

49

When Rose saw Cynthia returning to the guest room in the

early evening, she invited her in for a drink of coffee. Cynthia explained that Peter had evening classes, and, as she did not want to be locked out again, she had decided to come back early.

"And what do you think of life out here?" Rose asked her.

"It would take some getting used to," Cynthia replied – the food, the language, the traffic and all that. It is all so different from life back home."

"That's what I thought at first; then it gradually became normal."

"I suppose I would get used to it in time. Peter's awful busy, isn't he?"

"He is very conscientious. Believes in doing everything properly."

"That's the problem. I've come all this way and he doesn't seem to have enough time for me."

"I don't think he means to neglect you. It's just that he can't help having classes. He has to go and teach whether he has visitors or not."

"We had a nice day out on Wednesday," Cynthia admitted.

"Yes, I heard about that. You went to Blue Lake, didn't you?"

"Yes, that was good. There is some fabulous scenery here in

this country. I wish there was time to see a lot more of it."

"You should have come in vacation time. I'm sure Peter would have taken you on a grand tour."

"But, of course, I'm hardly the normal tourist type. I came here for one thing only, and that was to explore our relationship."

"Yes, I gathered that was the case. How's it working out?"

"It isn't really. I don't think it has brought us any closer together."

"I'm sorry to hear that." Yes, she could genuinely feel concerned.

"We just haven't had enough time together. We did some talking the other day, but we need to be able to relax and talk more."

"I'm sure he wants to do that. It's just that he has so many other calls on his time."

"And then there's – no, maybe I had better not say it."

"Go ahead. Say what is on your mind."

"This may be out of order. Well, what I was going to say is, I think he's fond of <u>you</u>."

Rose blushed at this unexpected suggestion. "What makes you say that?"

"No special reason. I've seen the way he looks at you, the way he relates to you."

"I hadn't noticed anything."

"I'm usually pretty good at reading minds."

"But he's never said anything; and, in any case, he had that arrangement with you."

"I would hardly call it an arrangement. We had a relationship at one time; then it went on hold. There has never been any real commitment."

"But I thought you came here to see if you had a future together. I would never seek to interfere."

"I'm not accusing you of that. But if it does not work out between the two of us, I would not be surprised if he should show more interest in you."

"I have not given him any encouragement." As she said this, Rose reflected that the idea of a closer relationship with Peter was appealing to her, no matter how much she tried to brush it off.

"I am not accusing you of anything. I am just trying to read the signals, that's all."

"I did not realize I was sending out any signals."

"Not purposely. However, give us time. Peter and I have to

talk this out some more. I hope that by the time I go home in a few days' time we shall have decided whether our relationship is on or off. At present I don't entertain high hopes for us, to put it bluntly."

"Allow yourselves a bit more time. After all, you've only been here a few days."

"I know; but it's been quite revealing already." Suddenly she changed the subject. "It can't be easy for you living alone like this."

"I'm used to it. I've never had a serious boy friend." That was one thing she regretted. There had, of course, been casual friendships, but these did not count.

"You deserve one. You're a good person." Rose could tell that Cynthia meant this. "You would make a good wife and mother. I told you I was a judge of character."

"You have really surprised me."

"I have seen that American woman – Miss Zimmer is it, you call here? I can't imagine you growing up to be like her."

"I don't want to be. She is a relic from the past – the kind of all-sufficient, all-competent missionary who can't put a foot wrong. I'm not like that. I'm a living human being with lots of needs, and I make mistakes" Once the words were out of her mouth, she felt that she had been unkind.

"Including the needs of husband and family."

"I wasn't going to say that."

"But it's implied, isn't it? I don't think you were cut out to be a spinster."

"In becoming a missionary I had to resign myself to such a possibility."

"It doesn't have to be like that."

"Of course, I'm open to all the Lord has for me."

"Whether you are married or single?"

"Why, yes."

"Then I'm suggesting you are the kind of person who should be married."

"I must confess that I am surprised at the way our conversation has gone. All I wanted to do was to help you and Peter to get a clear picture of God's guidance for you both."

"And that is what we are looking for. But it may not be what we were expecting at one time." She laid down her cup. "I'm sorry if I've embarrassed you. We Northerners like to be direct, don't we? It isn't very far between Blackburn and Manchester."

When Cynthia left, Rose's head was in a whirl. The last thing she wanted to do was to come between Peter and Cynthia. And yet..

50

The summons came the next morning. As she approached the principal's room, Alleyne wondered whether it would be another false alarm. As she walked, she found herself thinking again about Helen's murder. She still felt that the cook, Mr. Yu, was the culprit. On that brief acquaintance, she had not liked the look of him. How Helen could stand having him around she would never know. The very fact that he had fled was enough evidence of his guilt. It was to be hoped that he would soon be caught, so that justice could be done.

This time Dr. Lee was sitting at his desk. He rose as she entered the room and motioned to her to sit in the facing chair.

"You can probably guess why I asked to see you", he began. He spoke in English, even though she would have been perfectly happy if he had used Taiwanese.

"I guess it's about my future."

"Yes. I thank you for your patience."

Patience? She had felt anything but patient. What was wrong with the man? This whole thing had been drawn out far too long already. The sooner a decision was made the better, then with the help of her mission Alleyne could make plans.

"We have valued so much your contribution to the school," he opened. She had expected him to start this way. When the Chinese had bad news to give you they always started with praise. He would get round to the negative stuff when it suited him. As he spoke, he was twisting a pen round in his hands, a sure sign that he was embarrassed about the current situation. "You have given long and valuable service. Generations of students are grateful for all you have taught them." He put down the pen and began to clasp and unclasp his hands, which, if anything, was even more disconcerting.

"I have always given of my best," she said simply.

"And we are immensely grateful to you for that. But, of course, times change and priorities with them. Sometimes there is need to change our syllabus, and the particular classes you have taught will no longer be offered in the same format."

Why must he be so long winded? And why assume that she was not capable of altering the content of her lectures if needed? It would be easier if he simply said, "We don't want you any more". She decided to help him. "You are saying that there is no longer any work for me to do here?"

For a moment this interruption of his prepared speech stalled him. Then he continued, "That sounds rather negative, Miss Zimmer. It is time for a reappraisal, and it seems your talents might be better used elsewhere."

"But not in this college?"

"Under present conditions, no. I shall write to your mission with a glowing report and, no doubt, they will be able to redeploy you in some suitable way."

"You are aware, Dr. Lee, that I am approaching the end of my missionary service? Though not by choice, I assure you."

"Yes, Miss Zimmer, I am quite aware of that. It is therefore a good time to face something a little less challenging."

So he thought she was getting past it, did he? "Dr. Lee," she asserted, "I'm not in my dotage yet."

"Nobody suggested---"

"And I believe I still have much to give. I had not anticipated that I would need to change my job at such a late stage of missionary service; however, I see I am not in a position to fight against this."

"It is not a question of fighting anything, Miss Zimmer, but more a case of seeking the Lord's will for the rest of your service."

That's right, spiritualize it in order to make it sound better.

"We will have a special ceremony to record our thanks to you for all those years of faithful service."

That sounded like a face-saving effort. It was simply a polite way of getting rid of her.

"I don't want to hear how you are going to do it. It seems that everything has been decided and I must do as I am told."

"Miss Zimmer, there is nothing personal in all this. He had

picked up the pen again, but it slid through his fingers and dropped with a clatter. "I hoped you would see that it is all a part of the process of deciding what is best for the college." And also what suits the whims of a controversial principal. She rose to her feet. "If that is all, Dr. Lee, I have other things to do."

He rose and shook her limply by the hand. She was glad to get out of the room without showing her bitterness and resentment.

51

Early each morning, Peter would unlock the outer door of his home so that Simon could gain entrance. Ever since his conversion a few days earlier, Simon had been eager to spend as much time as possible studying the Word of God and growing in his new faith. As this would have been difficult to do in a room which he shared with three other students, Peter allowed him to use one of the rooms in his own building. It was such a thrill to see a young student who was so eager to grow in his new-found faith.

As for himself, he had attended one other evening of the special meetings, taking with him three of the students from the hostel, but there had been no similar response. Although the American evangelist was a powerful speaker, Peter could not help feeling that a Chinese evangelist, who understood local customs and thought patterns, could have preached in a more relevant way. However, he could not deny that the response up to now had been very good.

On this particular morning, before going to collect Cynthia, he was marking some assignments. Maybe it had not been a good plan to ask his day students to write essays just before Cynthia arrived on her visit, for they took a long time to mark, and his time with Cynthia was restricted. He had asked the students, when describing Wordsworth's poems, to use their own ideas; but time and time again the essays were simply a regurgitation of what he had told them in class. This was the Chinese way of doing things: the teacher was always right. So the study of literature and the study of science were little different: it was simply a matter of recalling the facts which the teacher had given them.

As he set off on the short walk to the college, he pondered the current situation. Although he could sense some of the old love that he had for Cynthia, he found it hard to imagine spending the rest of his life with her. He did not want to wound her, for she had taken all this trouble to come out and visit him, yet he was coming more and more to the conclusion that their relationship should end here.

It took him a while to cross the road, as the traffic was very heavy; and even when he thought he had spotted a clear space, a motor bike came roaring up and swerved to avoid him. Walking in Taiwan was a survival course, but he was used to it by now.

They had planned a walk together in a park that was not far away. It would have to be short, as Peter had a class shortly after 11. He felt bad about this, but Cynthia had to accept that there were obligations which he must fulfil.

She was just coming out of Rose's quarters, where she had had breakfast. He was so grateful for Rose's help, which was proving so valuable. Cynthia greeted him warmly. "Just need to go back and brush my teeth," she said. "I won't keep you long."

Soon they were walking down the street together. They passed a temple.

"You never take me to one of those," she said.

"I always try to avoid temples," he replied. "I went in one once, and there was a spirit medium there. I could sense a real spirit of evil, and I couldn't wait to get out. I don't want to repeat the experience, so I avoid temples altogether."

"Maybe you just picked a bad one."

"Is there such a thing as a good one? I prefer to look at them from the outside. That is good enough for me."

"If you say so, boss." She had not called him by that name before. It was hardly a term of endearment.

They reached the entrance to the park. Inside, there were still a few people doing their morning exercises. If it had been an hour earlier, there would have been many more of them. "They look so graceful," Cynthia commented.

"Yes, this is their daily routine. Chinese parks have been full of this sort of thing for centuries."

"Back home you might get the odd jogger, but that's all."

"We have joggers here too, but not many. Most prefer these traditional exercises. They know how to look after their bodies. You don't see many people who are obese."

"Can we sit down?" Cynthia said suddenly. "I want to share something."

There was a convenient bench, so they sat there.

"There's something I wanted to say to you," she said. "Perhaps I should have said this before, Peter, but I wanted to spend time with you getting to know you again and see how much of the old magic remained."

"Was there much of it?"

"Some," she admitted, "but that's not the whole story."

"Then what is the whole story?"

"I've been seeing someone."

This came as a complete surprise; and yet he had to admit that it would have been difficult for her to avoid all other relationships in the light of her ambiguous relationship with himself. "Tell me more".

"He is a teacher and he goes to our church."

"What is his name?"

"Oh, David. He teaches PE of all things."

"Is he dishy?" As soon as he said this, he regretted it; but Cynthia did not seem to mind.

"He is rather. Very sporty. He would be quite at home with all these folk doing their exercises."

"How long have you known him?"

"I've seen him around church for ages. We only began to go out together about six months ago. We seem to get on really well."

"Have you told him about us?"

"Of course. I wanted to be honest with him from the start."

"And what did you say?"

"I told him that we had been going together, and that I was not sure how it was going to work out."

"I am glad you were honest with him. What was his reaction?"

"He wanted to know more about you and whether we still felt close to one another."

"And what did you say?"

"I told him I wasn't sure how I felt any more. We talked about it quite a lot, and then, out of the blue, he suggested I should come over here to see you."

"So it was his idea, not yours?"

"He suggested it, but then it seemed a good idea to me too. You can say we decided it together."

"Wow, that's certainly something new to take on board. What are you going to tell him when you get back?"

"Peter, I'm still very fond of you, and I think you are of me; but I don't think it's going to lead to marriage."

"I was feeling rather like that myself."

She sighed. "It is such a relief to have got that out of the way. Now we can just be friends and enjoy the rest of my time here."

"Yes, I want you to really enjoy the next few days."

They got up and continued their walk.

52

It was the last night of the evangelistic meetings. Arnold was preparing to go there for the last time.

"I wish you didn't have to go out again," Kathleen said as they wiped the dishes together.

"After tonight we get back to normal."

"I'm so glad. I miss you dreadfully and so do the boys. There is no daddy to read them their bedtime story."

"Maybe I can read them two a night to make up."

When he went to say goodnight to the boys they were watching a programme on their small black and white TV set. "What is that programme?" has asked them.

"Syau fei sya", Philip replied.

"What is that?"

Kathleen explained: "It's a Japanese cartoon series."

"Looks a bit violent to me, sure it does."

"I'll keep an eye on it. If it gets too bad I'll switch it off."

"Oh Mum!" Philip interjected.

"Family hug?" Arnold suggested. The boys needed no second bidding. Arnold was so grateful to have such a loving family.

He drove the van to the venue, as he had several boxes of books with him. He liked to arrive early so as to set everything up in good time and to be available to early visitors. Sure enough, there were a number of early browsers this evening. People were particularly interested in two books by the speaker which had been translated into Chinese.

As he waited for people to show interest, Arnold's thoughts wandered. He could see a change in Kathleen since the accident, and this worried him. As for himself, he was growing more and more discontented with this job. He wanted to be out and about more, and using his journalistic skills. It was good that they would be going away on furlough in a few months' time; but it was not clear whether they should return or not. Until recently, he had not doubted that they would do so.

After the first 20 minutes he was joined by Frank, who had promised to help him. "I made it!" he announced, smiling.

"I'm glad you could come," Arnold welcomed him. "It looks as if it's going to be a busy evening. The prices are all marked; but if you have any problems just ask me."

"I will do."

"Did you manage to arrange to be free on Wednesday?"

"Yes, I asked at the college and they say they were happy for me to go."

"That's good news. We hope to go to Yunglin and Beitswun. It will be helpful to have someone else to talk with the customers – and even to keep me awake when I'm driving."

"Oh, I can do that. They say that I'm good at talking."

"Then you should be a valuable help."

When a prospective customer approached Frank with some

questions, Arnold left him to it, as such experience would be good for him.   It was at that moment that Pastor Fan came up to him. "It is going well, isn't it?" he beamed.

"Yes, there seems quite a lot of interest."

"Praise the Lord!" Just then Pastor Fan noticed Frank, and his expression changed. "Is that young man with you?"

"Yes, he's giving me some help."

"How well do you know him?"

"Not very well. He is a seminary student and he has offered to help me from time to time."

"Yes, I know who he is. All I can say to you is be careful. He could be trouble."

"Trouble? What do you mean?"

"I don't want to say any more. Just be careful, that's all."

As Pastor Fan walked away, no longer his normally ebullient self, Arnold wondered what the problem was.

BOOK FOUR : SEPTEMBER 1962

53

The time had come at last. Here she was at the valedictory service in her Blackburn church, and in two days' time she would be in Southampton, boarding a ship for the long voyage to Singapore.

The two years at Bible College had passed very quickly. She had made good friends there, and two of them would be sailing with her. She still remembered the words of her tutor, Miss Price, on the last evening. "Well, Rose, the adventure is just beginning. You are close to God's heart, for you have followed his will up to this point. Remember that your whole life is at his disposal. Make sure it stays that way. Most girls like to think they will one day have a husband and children, but that is by no means guaranteed for you. There are far more single girls than single men on the mission field. By agreeing to go out like this, you are committing yourself to the very real possibility that you will remain single for the rest of your life. For some, this is a great sacrifice, but God promises that he will be more than husband and children to you. Put him first, and you will never have cause to regret it."

Somehow, during those two years away, her Blackburn accent had become less pronounced, as if she was already beginning to be a citizen of the wider world.

During the service, she kept remembering the words of her

tutor. What was she really committing herself to? After the course in Singapore, she would be heading for Taiwan to a work as yet unknown. There was a very real possibility that Miss Price's words would prove prophetic. In her inner heart, however, she hoped that Miss Price would be proved wrong. She wanted to believe that, if she was loyal to God, he would reward her with the husband and children that she longed for.

In her talk she said all the right things: God had assured her of his call and she had obeyed; she had applied to the missionary society and been accepted; it was they who had suggested that Taiwan was the place for her; now she went out not knowing what the future held, but assured that God had a good purpose for her.

The congregation responded with warmth. The minister and the elders laid hands on her and prayed. There were murmurs of approval from members of the congregation. And yet, in the midst of all this there was a sense of unreality, as if all this was happening to someone else, not to herself.

The inevitable refreshments followed. This gave an opportunity for people who had known her for most of her life to come up and have a few words with her. Some said they would miss her, some said they were delighted for her, some said with a little trepidation that they hoped she would be safe, some referred to the difficulty of learning the language, some sought God's blessing on her, but one or two had some deeper insights to share.

One friend said: "Somehow I can't imagine you out there. You've always been such a fun person. Missionaries always seem to me to be such straightlaced people."

"Maybe then," Rose replied, "I can start a new trend."

Another said: "You fitted so well into this local situation. I can't imagine you in a place so far away with such different customs. I hope it won't be too hard for you."

"If I can adapt to Bible College, I should be able to adapt to that."

Another said, "It will be lonely for you, being so far from home."

Rose countered this with: "I shall make it my home. Just because I was born and grew up here, it doesn't mean that I can't feel at home somewhere else."

It was quite late when the proceedings came to an end and the minister gave her a last handshake of encouragement. The family returned home still buzzing with the excitement of the occasion.

Over cocoa they continued to talk together.

"I remember when you first got that bike," Mum said, "and I told you not to go so far again. I didn't think as you'd be going right across the world."

"Things were very different then. I've grown up, Mum, and I see things very differently. Although I'll be a long way off, my heart will still be here with you."

"A suppose you'll be needing a bike to get around when you land there," Dad said. "I could've got you a nice one. A pity you'll be so far away."

"Yes, I expect I *will* need a bicycle; but I'm sure there will be plenty available at a price I can afford."

"A wouldn't be surprised if it was a red one," Dad interjected.

"I wish *I* was going," her sister said. "It'll be boring here without you."

"You'll find plenty to do, sis. You might even settle down and start a family. You won't have time to be bored."

"It's too early yet," her sister complained. "I'm not ready for all that."

The next morning she took the train to London. There were, as expected, tears from her mother as they embraced for the last time. Dad pretended that he did not have any emotions, but it still showed. A neighbour who was the proud owner of a car took her to the station; then she was on her own. Another friendly neighbour, who had promised to wave from her garden as the train went past, kept her word. She was the last person from her old life whom Rose saw before the train took her away into her new life.

54

Alleyne was just returning from a lecture with books under her arm when Miss Huang from the office stopped her.

"Can we talk?"

"Of course. You mean now?"

"Yes. I'm worried."

"What is it then?"

"Can we go somewhere quiet?"

"We can go to my room."

As she turned her key in the lock there was a muted woof from Bessie, her black mongrel bitch. It was as if she was afraid to disrupt the air with too loud a bark. "She won't hurt you," Alleyne assured her visitor. When they were both seated, she said, "Now, what's the problem?" Secretly, she felt glad that Miss Huang felt free to take her into her confidence.

Her visitor seemed agitated. "May I speak in Taiwanese?"

"Of course you may."

"It's about the office," she began.

"Something wrong there?"

"You know I only go in three times a week. It is Mr. Liu who runs the place."

"Yes, I know him. Liu Ming Chi. He's only been with us for a few months, hasn't he? He seems friendly enough, though I don't know much about him really. Have you had problems with him?"

Miss Huang hesitated. "We have to keep a lot of loose money in the office. People bring in money for various things, and we need to have a certain amount to make out cash payments. We keep the money safely under lock and key, of course. And then we keep careful accounts. We have to keep an accurate record of all incomings and outgoings."

"And I am sure you must handle that job very well, my dear."

"That's the problem. Just recently it has been difficult to balance the books. Every so often there is money missing that we can't account for. I mentioned the problem to Mr. Liu. He said it was difficult to be absolutely accurate, and said we should just alter the figures. I felt bad about that, but he said it was the only way to handle the matter. After that I was all the more careful to make the figures match; but still there was money going missing. Mr. Liu said that it was only a matter of small sums and that we should not worry about it."

"It sounds a bit suspicious. You did right to come to me."

"But there is more. One morning I arrived early. When I opened the door he did not see me at first. I noticed that the money drawer was open and that he was putting something into his pocket."

"He was stealing, you mean?"

"Yes. It was very obvious. I pretended I had not noticed. I don't think he was aware that I had seen him and he acted normally."

"When was this?"

"Yesterday. I've been worried ever since. I had to tell someone."

"You did right to come to me."

"I am so worried. I don't know what to do. Shall I tell the principal?"

"I think you need to do more than that. This is a police matter."

"Really? But it is not a big matter. The principal should be able to handle it. Maybe he will dismiss Mr. Liu."

"This man has committed a crime. He needs to be exposed."

"But what about the college?"

"The college is not at fault. It is he who has broken the law."

"But it could ruin his career."

"He should have thought of that earlier."

"Couldn't we just settle it here in the college?"

"If we treat him too lightly he is more likely to offend again. If he gets punished, he is less likely to repeat his dishonesty. We are really helping him to live a good life."

"I had not seen it that way. If you say so."

"You know that I only have his good at heart."

"I suppose so."

"I am glad you came to me. We can soon sort this out."

55

It would soon be time for Peter to return to his theological college and for his friend Geoffrey to go back to his teacher training college. They had both developed a liking for fell walking. Having been born and reared in Keswick they were admirably placed to develop this hobby. As Geoffrey had obtained the use of his dad's car for the day, they drove to Thirlmere, and from there began their conquest of Helvellyn.

As neither of them had done this climb for a long time, they relied heavily on a map and also on a book by an enthusiast called Wainwright. Although the climb was demanding, it was well within their capabilities. It was only when they got to Striding Edge that it became at all threatening. On either side of the path which they followed, there was a sheer drop It did not help when they saw a memorial to someone who had fallen to his death and been guarded by his faithful dog even when the breath had left his body.

It had been sunny when they set out, but now there was some hint of mist. Thankful to have got past Striding Edge safely, they climbed a steeper slope, expecting to reach the peak; but when they got there they found there was another peak just ahead of them. It was a relief when they came to what appeared to be the real summit; though they were disappointed that the growing mist deprived them of the view which they had earned by their efforts.

There they sat for a while, hoping that the mist would soon lift in order to facilitate the return journey.

"Well, at least," Geoffrey said, "if anything happens to you, Pete, your dad is a doctor and he should be able to help."

"He's not an orthopaedic specialist, and, in any case, he would probably be too busy helping others."

"Do you really think that?"

"It doesn't surprise you, does it? He works all hours, and I feel as if I hardly know him. He has always been like that. And Mum lives under his shadow. She was never a person I could get very close to."

"So different from my own parents," Geoffrey said. "We were always a very close family, as you know; and they have given me every encouragement to pursue a teaching career. What did your parents think about your choice of a career?"

"A bit negative at first. My father had hoped that I would go into medicine like himself. When he had got used to the idea of my entering the ministry, he was more resigned to it; though he has never given me any practical encouragement."

"You must make a good minister," Geoffrey assured him.

"What makes you say that?"

"Well, you're good with people. In fact, you're more like my parents than yours. You make time for others. They will love you."

"I hope you're right. I want to give myself to others, but I would like to have a good home life as well."

"Then you really do want to be like my parents rather than yours."

"Exactly. I wouldn't like my children – if I ever have any – to feel I had no time for them."

"I don't think that is very likely."

"I wonder. I have my parents' genes in me. Maybe I'll be so caught up in other people's lives that I won't have time to marry and bring up a family."

"I don't think that's very likely."

"We shall soon find out. In any case, I am not thinking of marrying early. I want to understand my job properly before I think of things like that."

"Do you know where you will work?"

"Not yet. I'll probably start looking for a place to serve my first curacy soon. I shan't be ordained for a year yet. I will probably move to another curacy three years down the line; then after that, it's anyone's guess."

"Ever thought of going abroad?"

"Not really; though they did ask me at college to be missionary secretary. I don't know why. Maybe they were hard up."

"Don't put yourself down, Pete. You're the sort of person who could do anything. If you went abroad you would make a success of it."

"I would only go if I felt a real sense of call. Otherwise, it's ministry in this country for me."

"And you'll make a success of it, mark my words."

Peter looked around him. "I think the mist is lifting. Shall we make a start on the descent?"

56

On the second day of his vacation at Sun Moon Lake, Arnold had done the usual tourist thing: he had visited an Aboriginal settlement and seen the natives in their national costume. They posed for photographs with their grass huts in the background; but he was perfectly aware that when the tourists had left they would revert to normal civilized living. They even had colour television. He would like to write a satirical article about them, but it was probable that nobody would want to read it.

What was he doing in Taiwan anyway? His first two years had been taken up with language study, a task for which, as he had suspected, he found he had no great aptitude. However, the hard work had paid off. When that period was over it was decided that church work was the best niche for him. He was attached to a church in the suburbs of Taichung, where he was supposed to be responsible for youth work. The young people were a giggly lot, who valued him chiefly as someone with whom they could practise their English.

At the games evenings, he was responsible for giving a short talk, which it took him ages to prepare. He felt like a fish out of water; but maybe, after his furlough the following year, he would be able to find some work which was more suited to his talents.

As he sat in the little pavilion with a view across the lake, an elderly Westerner came to sit beside him. He wondered whether he was supposed to know him. It was a trifle embarrassing. Each waited for the other to speak.

"My name's Dick – Dick Spurling," the other man ventured.

The name rang a bell. He was a veteran missionary, who had spent many years on the Mainland before moving to Taiwan, and he had a reputation for telling dramatic stories from the past.

"Yes, I've heard about you," Arnold replied. "You've got quite a reputation."

"I was just doing my job. Sometimes it was by no means easy. But I stuck at it. The Lord was good. China was a rollercoaster toward the end. Hard to adapt to Taiwan but I made it. Had a great wife, Greta."

"Had?"

"She died two years ago. All good things come to an end. But I still survive."

"You must be due to retire soon."

"I go back at the end of this year. It's going to be hard. This is the only life I have known."

"Where is home?"

"Here, of course. But I shall find myself stuck in some village just outside London where my brother lives."

"That must be hard for you, sure it must."

"No need to ask where you come from," the man smiled.

"Is it so obvious?"

"I'm afraid it is. You a missionary too?"

"Yes, of sorts. I was a journalist before, and I am missing it already. I am fairly new here: I don't have your experience."

"Time will change you. I hope you make a good success of it."

They were silent for a while. Arnold tried to reflect on all the changes which his companion must have faced down the years. It would make a good book. How he would like to write such a book!

But there was no invitation to do so, and all his attention was focused on retaining the language and trying to relate to Chinese young people in some meaningful way.

The older man got up with a word of apology and made off to some unknown destination. Arnold took up the crime novel that he had brought with him and opened it at page one. He had reached page two when two girls came and sat in another part of the pavilion. Although they were Westerners, they carried parasols, so that, like their Chinese counterparts, they could escape the worst ravages of a blazing sun.

It was love at first sight. The girl with the pale blue dress, the red parasol and the jet black hair caught his attention at once. The other girl he hardly noticed. They were busy talking with each other and did not appear to notice him. He knew he had to make contact.

Rather than make it too obvious, he decided to hail them from where he was. "Hi," he said. "My name is Arnold and I'm from Belfast."

The girl with the blue dress was the one to reply. "I'm Kathleen Mason," she responded, and I live in a suburb of London you've probably never heard of. And this is Jean Fellowes, who comes from Hull, but is not very proud of it."

"I didn't say that," the other girl retorted.

"Are you just on a trip?" Arnold asked.

"No, we're those dreadful people called missionaries. At least, we think we are, but we haven't had a lot of opportunity to try it out yet. "

"I'm a missionary too, but feel as if I'm still cutting my teeth."

He wanted this conversation to last much longer. How could he achieve that? He had an idea. "There's a nice little coffee shop just down the road," he said. "Could I treat you both to something?"

"Sounds fun," Kathleen responded.

They walked together to the café. Arnold felt a bit shaky, as he had never been controlled by such emotion before. What was happening to him? Was this going to prove a significant moment in his life?

BOOK FIVE : JUNE 1972

57

The summer heat was fierce. With temperatures rising to 97 degrees Fahrenheit every day, it was hard to avoid perspiration. Forgoing her walks, Rose was content to sit in the courtyard under the shade of a banyan tree, reading a book while a gentle breeze wafted her body. Even when she did go out, she armed herself with a parasol, like her Chinese counterparts, as protection against the fierce sun. As it was examination time, her services in the classroom were no longer required.

Since Peter and Cynthia had split up, there was a stronger possibility of forging a deeper relationship with Peter. At the same time, she recalled how people, before they met, had already determined to throw them together, and for that reason she was wary. If the two of them were meant to be together, surely God would make it obvious.

They met chiefly at the Sunday evening gathering with the other missionaries, and cycled back together as a matter of course. Last Sunday Peter had mentioned that two buttons had come loose from his trousers, and she had offered to sew them on for him. When he collected them, he had been most grateful. This, however, was hardly the sign of a deeper relationship. She must admit that a love for him was growing, but it was normally expected that the man would make the first move, and so far Peter had not done that.

Miss Zimmer came walking past, but her only greeting was a slight nod. Rose felt sorry for her, as her future was so uncertain. She was still waiting for some indication from her missionary society as to how they hoped to use her during the last part of her missionary service. It was obvious that she dreaded being given a job back in the USA, far from her Chinese friends. Although she was not the sort of person to inspire a lot of sympathy, Rose on this occasion felt genuinely sorry for her.

She resumed reading her book. It was a devotional book, but her mind was wandering so much that she derived little help from it.

Sometimes she wondered how she had got herself into this situation. It sounded so dull working with girls in an Asian seminary. A part of her wanted to live a life of fun and excitement. Her friends had been very surprised when she had entered Bible School and gone to the ends of the earth to work for God; but that was a long time ago, and she had got used to this situation. Some of them had duller lives, simply keeping to routine and bringing up their children. She did not envy them that.

The silence was shattered when Florence came running up in a state of severe agitation. "Oh, Li Lausu, I've been looking for you everywhere."

"Why, whatever is the matter?"

"It's my sister – she's had an accident."

"What kind of an accident?"

"She was riding with her boy friend on a scooter. I don't know what happened. Maybe it was a cat in the road. They had to swerve, and she fell off. It looks as if she has broken a leg."

"Where is she now?"

"At the hospital. My mother just called to tell me. She's my only sister. I'm so worried."

"Do you want me to go to the hospital with you?"

"Please, Li Lausu. I'm afraid to go alone."

"And you've no exams today?"

"No."

"Then we had better go. I presume it is the local hospital."

"Yes. We could go on the bus. It is only about five stops."

"I know where it is. Just give me a few moments, Florence, and we will go together."

Florence was not the sort of person to cope well with emergencies, and for this reason Rose knew that her presence was essential.

58

Although three months had gone by, nothing had changed. Alleyne did not consider herself to be an impatient person, but this long wait was becoming hard to bear.

Why had the police in all that time failed to apprehend the cook, Mr. Yu? She still felt that he was the obvious suspect. He must have known there was money in the house, yet, as far as she was able to determine, no money had been found. He must have stabbed her to death, seized the money and made his escape. She had even visited the police station to voice her suspicions in the hope that this would lead to a speedy arrest; but there was no indication that they had taken any action at all. It was so frustrating.

One day, on a whim, she had visited the area. She had stood for a while looking at the house, with the pool in front of it, and recalled those happier days when Helen was alive. Until the culprit was arrested and charged, there would be no closure.

There had also been no further news of what would happen to her in the future. She was due to leave on furlough in three weeks' time, and there was no indication yet as to what the mission wanted her to do. It was her fervent hope that there would be other work for her to do in Taiwan. She had even suggested some possibilities to them. All she met with, however, was either a wall of silence or an assurance that the matter was being taken care of. That was not good enough.

She did not know whether she would have to put her goods into storage. If she should be relocated back to the USA, she would get rid of most of her possessions and only take back the essentials. The idea of living there, however, appalled her. Throughout her life she had lived in a Chinese environment. Despite her visits on furlough, the USA was like a foreign country to her. She had neither friends nor family there.

The other problem was what to do with her dog, Sandy. The two of them were closely attached to each other. She wanted to stay in Taiwan and continue to take him for his walks. Sandy was also someone to talk to, to share her innermost thoughts. He always received these messages with rapt attention and wagged his tail in agreement with her. If she were to return to the States, Sandy would have to be left behind. Hopefully she would be able to find a new owner; but if not.... She did not like to consider this possibility.

Daily she scanned the newspapers for news of the murder investigation. Her Chinese was good enough to ensure that she missed nothing. However, the editors obviously considered that it was past news and of no further interest to anyone. Daily also she visited the office to collect her mail; but there was nothing whatsoever about her future.

"I'll let you know, Sz Lausu, as soon as we receive anything," Alice in the office assured her, sensing her concern for the future.

Some of the students had begun their exams, and there were already some papers for her to mark. She was glad of this, as it took her mind off these other matters. It saddened her, however, to reflect that this would be the last time she would perform such a duty.

On this morning she sat in her room, shortly after nodding to Rose, took out her red pen, and began the task.

Within a few days both matters would be resolved, but not in ways which she might have expected.

59

It was lunchtime at the hostel again. Old Su had produced as one of his dishes a combination of egg and tomato. Such a meal was well within the pockets of cash-strapped students. He would prepare more meat dishes on occasions when he was given extra money. Looking around Peter could see a few empty places. This examination period caused some changes.

"Finished your exams yet?" he asked Mark, who nodded an affirmative.

"How do you think you've done?"

Mark shrugged. "Not so difficult. Should pass, I think."

"And then your study overseas?"

"After military service, yes. If I haven't forgotten how to study by then."

Wang Ming had just been helping himself to extra rice. "No more teaching for you?"

"Not this term, no."

"So you can relax."

"Not really. This is marking time."

"Well, you can relax afterwards. Time to go out with your girl friend."

"My girl friend?"

"You know, the one at the seminary. She fancies you."

"How do you know that?"

"I can tell. I've seen you together."

"We are friends, yes, but it hasn't gone any further."

"Then it should. You would be good together."

Peter tried not to look as embarrassed as he felt. He looked around, hoping to change the subject.

"I don't see Paul today. He's usually back by now."

"Don't know where he is," Mark said. "I think he's finished his exams. I saw him going out on the bike."

"I wish I could afford a bike like that," Wang Ming complained.

"When you are earning money," Mark said, "you will be able to afford one."

It was Simon's turn to speak. "Are you still coming to meet my parents tomorrow?"

"Yes, of course," Peter assured him. "I promised, didn't I?"

"They don't know I'm a Christian yet. I will tell them when it seems right."

"You told me they only speak Taiwanese. That means I can't talk to them."

"I can translate. It's no problem. Or better still - "

"Yes?"

"Your friend, Rose. She speaks Taiwanese, doesn't she?"

"Yes, she does.""Then why not ask her to join us?"

Just as Peter was pondering this, Joshua came rushing in, alarm written all over his face. "Have you heard the news?" he cried out.

"What news?" Peter asked.

"It's Paul. He had a crash."

"Oh no. Is he hurt?"

"Jenny is. They took her to hospital."

There was general consternation among the students. Peter got up. "I must go and see her. Is she in the main hospital?"

"I think so."

"I'll let you know how things are when I get back."

"I could go with you," Joshua offered.

"No, you've got your exams. I don't mind going alone."

Peter got out his push-bike and began the fifteen minute ride to the hospital. He tried not to let his imagination run riot as he pedalled. There were so many accidents on the roads in this land that the only surprise was that this had not happened before.

60

Over the past three months, Arnold had got to know Frank much better. They had been on four trips together to the outlying villages. He had proved to be excellent at reaching out to local people. Time and again he was found to be sharing his faith with strangers.

If he had one fault, it was that he was very political. He was very critical of the current government, and such talk could get him into trouble. It was easy to see why he had been warned about this man. However, their relationship was not about political activity but about gospel outreach.

They had spent the morning at Pingyuan and enjoyed beef noodles with the Yangs. Now it was time to set off for Lanying again. On this trip, Frank was particularly talkative. Although the conversation was in Mandarin, Arnold found it easy to understand him.

"Did you read the book I lent you?" Frank asked him.

"Yes, I did. I must give it back to you."

"What do you think of it?"

"If it is all true---"

"It is true. The government doesn't want you to believe it, but it is true all right."

"It is hard to believe that the new government under Chiang Kai Shek would act so cruelly. After all, he calls himself a Christian."

"I suppose he thought there was no other way. People did not like him. He destroyed so much to try to win the war.. Then it did not work and he came here. He needs support from the Americans. He needs to show them who is leader. That is why he does bad things."

"But to kill all the leaders -"

"It is the only way to make himself strong. And it gives him power. All his enemies are destroyed."

"Were they really enemies?"

"He thought so."

"The Americans would never have given him all that aid if they had known."

"That was why it was kept a secret. Though people must have known about it."

"Yes, I suppose it suited them to regard him as a Christian president and maintain friendly relations with him. I don't see how the regime could have prospered without their help."

"And Chiang Kai Shek likes to let people think he is a Christian, though it is Madam Chiang who is the real Christian."

"Yes, I see all that. But it is hard to know what to do about it."

"You are a journalist, aren't you? Your job is to write about to the truth."

"I know I'm a journalist; but I'm also here as a Christian missionary. I may not agree with the way the Nationalists came to power; but if I try to expose them, that will be the end of my missionary career here."

"I see that you have a problem. There are a group of us working for independence. We believe the days of the

Nationalists are numbered."

"That is hard to conceive. Their power is so strong."

"Not for ever. I believe change will come."

"I admire your beliefs; but it is dangerous to express them."

"I know. That is a risk we have to take."

"And what do you propose to do?"

"What I am doing now. Telling other people the truth. I believe more and more people will come over to join us. The day will come when the Nationalists will lose control; then we shall be ready to take over."

"At the moment that is hard to believe."

"It is not going to happen tomorrow. But it will happen. And I don't think America will support this government for ever. The day will come when they will recognise Mainland China and forget Taiwan."

"Yes, I can believe that. There are not many countries that recognise Taiwan and not the Communist regime."

"That is what I mean. It can't go on like this. When Chiang dies, things will begin to change."

"I can believe that; but it is not wise to talk about it much at this stage."

"I think that, as a journalist, you ought to be be prepared to speak out."

"I told you, I am not here as a journalist. I am here as a missionary."

"Then it is important that you should not ignore what is going on."

He admired the earnestness of this young man, but felt concerned that his outspokenness would one day get him into trouble.

"We're almost at Lanying," he said.

61

Rose and Florence arrived at the hospital without much delay. It was not the sort of place Rose would care to visit if she was sick. The outer stonework was a dull grey, and it had been patched up in various places. Inside, it seemed that every room was a mixture of grey and green, but so begrimed that it was often hard to tell one from the other. In some spots the plaster had come away altogether. As soon as you went through the door there was a smell of ether, or something very like it.

The problem was how to find Florence's sister Jenny. The casualty department seemed the best place to begin. They went up to the reception desk and Florence made some enquiries. After a while she turned. "It looks as if she was taken straight into a cubicle."

"Are we allowed to go inside to see?"

"I can because I am her sister. Perhaps you would like to sit here while I look for her."

"Yes, that sounds like a good idea."

Rose took a seat. She had only been sitting there for a minute or so when a familiar figure walked in. "Why, Peter."

Peter was as surprised as she was. "Rose, what are you doing here?"

Rose looked thoughtful "Maybe we are here for the same reason."

For Peter, something clicked. "Is it about a scooter accident?"

"Yes. Was it one of your students that crashed?"

"Yes, but how do you know Jenny?"

"She is Florence's sister. Florence is one of our students."

"That explains it. I never knew that. I must admit I almost saw this coming. The way the girls sit side saddle, it's asking for trouble."

"I know. Somehow they think it is more respectable not to sit in a straddling position. The idea of danger does not seem to occur to them."

"Do you know how she is?"

"Florence has just gone in to find out. It seems Jenny has broken her leg."

"As long as it is no worse. It seems that Paul was not hurt."

"He was not sitting side saddle."

"Yes, that is a safer position to be in. I expect he is with her now."

"We will find out when Florence comes back."

Just then Florence reappeared. She too was surprised to see Peter.

"Well?" Rose asked.

"She was there. She is just waiting for a bed on the ward; then they will do the operation as soon as possible."

Rose translated for Peter. "What about Paul?" he asked.

"He wasn't there."

"But I thought he would have been with her."

Florence launched into an explanation, and Rose translated.

"Paul has been taken to the police station. They want to question him about this."

Peter looked indignant. "That is to treat him like a common criminal."

"That's the way they do things here," Rose said. "Who are we to judge?"

Peter sighed. "There are many things about life here that I find hard to take."

"Join the club," Rose said.

"I suppose I had better go to the police station to make contact. There is not much point in my staying here. You can keep me in touch." He stood up, but just before leaving he asked, "Oh, there is one more thing. You remember Simon, who became a Christian just recently?"

"Yes, I remember him clearly."

"I'm going to visit his folks tomorrow. They speak Taiwanese, and you might like to go with us."

"I would be glad to unless we are occupied with Jenny. Can we wait and see how things develop?"

As Peter left, Florence turned to Rose for a translation of the bits she had not understood. Then she said, "I am going to sit with Jenny again. If they are ready to let you in, I'll come back for you."

62

The knock at the door elicited a dutiful bark from Sandy. When Alleyne opened the door, she was surprised to see Inspector Nee standing there.

"They told me I would find you here," he explained.

"Yes. You're very welcome. Do come in."

When they were seated, he explained, "You must be wondering why I am here. There has been a development."

Alleyne's heart missed a beat. Had they caught Mr. Yu at last? "What sort of a development?"

"I expect you are aware of the pool just outside your friend's house?"

"Yes. It is a dangerous place. Children could fall in."

"More than that. A whole taxi."

"A taxi? Drove into the pool?"

"Yes. It was a wet day, and the road surface was covered with water. The pool must have just looked like a part of the road."

"But I don't see what this has to do with the murder."

"It has a lot to do with it. When they pulled the taxi out of the water they found something else."

Probably the murder weapon. Why must he take so long to explain? "Was it a knife?"

"No, nothing like that. It was the body of this cook, Mr. Yu."

Alleyne had not expected anything like this. "Are you sure it was Mr. Yu?"

"Of course. It has been identified. His body was full of stab wounds. His pockets were also filled with stones to make sure that he sank."

Alleyne for once was at a loss for words. This was the last thing she would have expected.

"It is, of course, not wise to speculate at this stage, but it seems to me that a thief broke in, your friend surprised him, and when he attacked her Mr. Yu came to the rescue. You saw him as the murderer, but I think we have to see him as a hero instead."

Alleyne's mind would not adjust to this sudden transition.

"I have come to see you in case you can throw any light on the subject. You were quick to blame Mr. Yu; but now that you know he was not responsible, do you have any other ideas? Can you think of anyone else who might know that your friend kept money in the house?"

"I doubt whether she told many people about it. I don't really have any idea. What will you do now?"

"We will continue our investigations. Now that Mr. Yu is no longer under suspicion, we will conduct some more fingerprint tests in the house itself. It is just possible that we may have a match in our records. Other than that, I have nothing to offer. Obviously, we do not share our methods extensively with the public, or the real criminal might hear about it."

"I quite understand. I am sorry I can't help you more on this. I have no idea who might be involved."

"Don't worry. I didn't really think you would have; but we like to check these things as thoroughly as possible."

"If I get any ideas, I will let you know." She had to say that, but the whole thing was a mystery to her.

63

When Peter arrived at the police station he asked the officer at the desk about Paul.

"He's been taken inside for fingerprinting and questioning. You'll have to wait here."

'Fingerprinting' was not in Peter's vocabulary, but the officer used gestures to make his meaning clearer. It annoyed him that he could not get alongside Paul at this time of need, but he had to do as he was told. He sat on a bench and waited. As he did so, he had plenty of time for his thoughts. He hoped Paul would be able to cope with all this. It was good that he had a firm faith: this should be of great help to him in the current circumstances.

He also found himself thinking of Rose. They had a lot in common. Both of them cared a lot for people and would go out of their way to help others. Rose was as devoted to her students at the seminary as he was to his students in the hostel. That was something they had in common. He liked her for the good qualities he saw in her, but now he knew there was something more. That 'liking' was gradually being transformed into 'love'. Now that Cynthia was no longer a part of the picture, he was free to develop this relationship more.

After about half an hour, Paul appeared. He sprang to his feet. "How was it?"

"Don't they care how I feel? I wanted to be with Jenny at the hospital but they wouldn't let me. It was all questions, questions, questions."

"What actually happened?"

"There was this motor bike on the wrong side of the road heading straight for us. I had to swerve to avoid it and Jenny fell off. That's all there is to it. But they asked me all those questions just as if I was the one at fault. They ought to be questioning that motorcyclist, but he got away and I don't think anyone can identify him."

"Are they charging you with anything?"

"No, I don't think so."

"Good. I'm sorry you've had all this to go through."

"They don't care. They can't see things from my standpoint."

"I suppose they feel they have their job to do."

"Now I must get to the hospital to see Jenny. Do you have any news of her?"

"She is going to have an operation very soon."

"You were there?"

"Yes, and so was Rose. She was with Jenny's sister, Florence."

"That was good of her."

"If we go to the hospital we may have to wait till she comes round from the operation."

"I don't mind. I'll wait as long as I need to."

"Let us go by taxi. It's quicker."

"But what about your bike?" He had noticed it leaning against the wall.

"It's locked. Should be safe until I come back for it."

"OK. Let's go then".

64

The old lady with the joss stick, bowing her head at the entrance to the temple, was so intent on her worship that she did not appear to notice Arnold. Frank was talking enthusiastically with a passer by. It had been a better than usual visit to Lanying. Several people had bought books, and there had been a number of enquirers about the faith. Soon it would be time to pack up and go home.

Just then a young girl came up. "Do you know me?" she enquired in Mandarin with a testing smile.

He looked at her more closely. "Did you come into the shop once or twice?"

"Yes. Do you know who I am?" While Arnold was trying to recall this, she went on, "I am Catherine. I was studying at the seminary. Rose is my friend and teacher."

"Ah yes, I remember now. We have been praying for you. I gather you were supposed to be getting married."

"That's right. So you do remember me."

"I do now. Are you married yet?"

"I have some good news," she said. "But I want to go back to Nancheng and tell people myself. You can tell them I am coming if you wish."

"This all sounds very mysterious."

"Not for long. They will be glad to receive my news. Now I must go. I have to cook food for the family." With these words she turned and left, leaving Arnold to contemplate what this good news might be.

A few minutes later the two of them were packing up. "That was a good visit," Frank exclaimed enthusiastically. That man I was talking to just now – I don't think he's far from being a Christian."

"Yes, I could see you were enjoying a good conversation."

When the packing was done, they climbed into the van and began the return journey. "I enjoy this work," Frank enthused. It is so kind of you to let me accompany you."

"You seem to be very good at taking opportunities."

"I like people," Frank replied.

"But not all people."

"What do you mean?"

"Your remarks about the government."

"Oh yes. That is a very different matter." He appeared to hesitate. "I wondered---"

"Yes?"

"There's a group of us that meets to discuss independence. Would you like to join us?"

Arnold's mind whirled. This was obviously an illegal organisation on which the government would wish to clamp down hard.

"I don't think it would be wise for me. It might interfere with my Christian work."

"I understand," Frank replied, though he seemed disappointed. As he drove on, Arnold thought about this. He hoped that Frank would not get himself into trouble.

65

Rose remained with Florence and her parents during the period of the operation; and when she learned that it had been performed successfully, she took her leave. Peter and the student Paul were still there when she did so.

The next day she went, as agreed, with Peter to the village where Simon's parents lived. As usual in the hot weather he was wearing shorts. He had nice legs; but was she justified in thinking this way? His yellow top did not go very well with the beige shorts, but it was not for her to criticize. They travelled by bus. As usual, all the seats were taken. When they were five minutes into the journey, the driver applied his brakes suddenly, and the standing passengers shot forward, only just managing to avoid collapsing in a heap. "I sometimes wonder if they do that on purpose," Peter commented.

At the bus stop they were met by Simon himself. "Welcome," he said in English. "My parents are looking forward to seeing you." He escorted them to the family home, which was a low roofed building set in its own yard. "Don't tell them about my faith. I will tell them when I think it is the right time. I know they will be very angry at first."

Simon's mother was standing at the door. She gave them an effusive welcome in Taiwanese. Rose decided that she did not need to translate for Peter, as her meaning was very obvious. She led them into the living room, where Simon's father, a somewhat gnarled figure, was sitting. The room was dominated by a large family shrine. His greeting was polite, but not as demonstrative as that of his wife. It was obvious that he was very pleased that Rose was able to speak to him in his own language. Indicating Peter, he queried, "Your husband?"

"No," Rose explained. "We are not married. We are just friends. Peter brought me because I speak your language."

"You speak it very well," the old man replied. Rose explained to Peter in a whisper about the mistake, and Peter saw the funny side of it.

Meanwhile, his wife offered them plates and indicated that they should help themselves to water melon and to pineapple. This was in the best tradition of Chinese hospitality. "We are honoured to welcome our son's teacher to our home," the mother said. Rose explained this to Peter. Teachers were regarded with great respect in Chinese circles.

Simon's father had disappeared, and he returned carrying a large tray which held a small teapot and four tiny cups. He beamed as he set this down on a table in front of the others. At this point Simon broke out coughing. He apologized for this. His mother looked a bit concerned.

"I hope my son is a good student," the father said. Rose translated for Peter, who said, "He is one of my best students."

Simon made some remark of disparagement. It was not regarded as good form to relish compliments.

"We hope he will be a good teacher one day," father said. "He will be able to influence many lives." A good education was a high priority in Taiwan at that time. Parents would make big sacrifices so that their children could enjoy this. Many students would go on to study abroad, usually in the USA. Looking round the house, which was cheaply furnished, Rose assumed that this would not be an option for Simon.

Then father returned to his old theme. "You are planning to get married?"

Rose felt a little embarrassed. "We don't know," she replied.

Simon's father seemed surprised at such a non-committal answer. "Everyone should get married," he declared. "It is the right thing to do." Rose saw that Simon was translating for Peter. This saved her any embarrassment.

"We hope our son can find a good wife," Mother went on.

"He has a good education. It should not be difficult."

Rose was surprised that they were not planning an arranged marriage for him. It was such a traditional household that she would have expected this. Perhaps Simon had made it clear that this was not his wish.

Suddenly Simon started to cough again. "You need some medicine," his mother announced.

"It is nothing special," Simon argued. "It will soon go away."

"When your friends have eaten, we will go to the market. Perhaps they would like to see it."

When Rose explained this to Peter he looked puzzled. She explained: "There is a kind of doctor at the market. People go to him for medicines."

"How do you know?"

"Because I've seen this sort of thing before."

There was no hurry. They continued to eat their fruit, and the cups of Chinese tea were refilled. Only when it seemed that they had had enough did the mother say, "And now we must go to the market."

"Why don't you come as well?" Simon invited. "You should find it interesting."

So that is what the

66

The long awaited letter had arrived. Alleyne collected it from the office and took it back to her quarters so that she could read it in private. Sandy looked up briefly from his slumbers, observed that a walk was not in the offing, and settled back to sleep.

Yes, it was the letter she had been expecting, sent from her mission's headquarters. Now she would learn of her fate. She had made it known that she wished to continue in Taiwan, and wondered what suggestions they would make for her last term of service there.

It began 'Dear Alleyne'. That sounded very informal. She preferred to be called 'Miss Zimmer'. She read on. "We have taken note of your wish to remain in Taiwan; and, indeed, we are very grateful for the valuable service you have given over the years both in Mainland China and in Taiwan. However, at this present time the mission does not have any openings in Taiwan which would be suited to your experience and expertise.

"At the same time, we have taken note of the increasing number of students from Taiwan who come to these shores for further study. At present we have nobody to work among them. Would you be prepared to initiate a ministry toward these overseas students in one of our major cities?"

Her first reaction was a feeling of disappointment. After a lifetime of living amongst the Chinese, she was to move to an

American environment. It would be like living in a foreign country. Of course, this was better news than she had dared to expect. At least, she would be spending a lot of time with Chinese people. She read on.

"Although you are nearing retirement, we note that you have had a lot of experience working with young people, and we know that they look up to you. Bearing this in mind, we have no hesitation in recommending that you pioneer this kind of work. Hopefully the mission will in due course recruit others. You will have a hand in training some of these. We hope you will consider this to be a work which fits well with your talents."

Yes, it was better than she might have hoped. All the same, the thought of leaving Taiwan this time and not returning depressed her. She would miss the life here. Working in a predominantly Western environment would be difficult for her.

She carried on reading. "We realize that this may not be your ideal choice of work; but there are no other constructive suggestions at present. Do let us know as soon as you can how you react to this suggestion. We hope that we can reach an amicable agreement and make the best use of your talents during this last tour of service."

The letter ended with the usual formalities. She dropped the letter on the table-top and began to work out the implications. Poor Sandy was lying in his basket unaware of the changes that lay ahead. What was she going to do with him? Was there anybody who would take good care of him? How she would miss him! Maybe she could get another dog, but it would not be the same. If her work should be itinerant, there would be problems too.

She had just a month left to work this out. Already she was beginning to feel the pangs of leaving. At other times she had been able to bear these absences because they were only temporary. This time it would be very final. She felt overwhelmed by a deep sadness.

67

As they walked to the market with Simon's mother, Peter could not help stealing glances at Rose. In a way, it was as if he had never seen her before. She had a good dress sense: the lilac top and purple trousers suited her: he had not noticed before how curvy she was.

At the market they found the usual fruit and vegetable sellers, the meat sellers and so on; but there were also some who squatted on a sheet on the floor waiting for their customers. It was to one of these that they went. The vendor himself had a long straggly beard which made him look like a Chinese from ancient times. Only his rough Western clothes belied this. On either side of him were people selling grain, and just behind him there was a shoe stall. He had with him a number of packets. Simon's mother explained what was wrong with her son, and the vendor nodded with understanding. Not far away a young boy was trying in vain to rein in a frisky puppy. On hearing of the complaint, the man produced from a large travelling bag two tins marked 'Best Tea'. Each contained a substance which resembled sand. He mixed the two together, gave some verbal instruction as to its use, and handed the packet over to Mother in exchange for a few coins.

It was so different from how they did things at home: you would book an appointment, be examined by the doctor, be given a prescription, and you would then take it to a chemist's to obtain the medicine. Here it was all done with the minimum of protocol. Simon said, "He is a very good doctor. My mother has great faith in him."

His mother beamed with satisfaction now that the task was accomplished. She said something to Rose, who translated for Peter: "She says that if ever you should be sick, this is a good place to come."

"Tell her I will remember that," Peter smiled.

They walked back to the house, which was not far away. When they were invited to go back inside, Peter and Rose took this as a good moment to leave. The two parents stood at the door waving farewell until they had turned a corner and were out of sight."

"They wouldn't be so friendly if they knew about Simon's conversion," Peter explained.

They came to the bus stop. Peter said, "I really feel I've got to know you so much better over the last two days."

"Yes, I've felt the same."

"It's not as if this was planned. It just seems to have

happened."

"But it could hardly be called romantic."

"What do you mean?"

"Visiting folk in hospital. Visiting Simon's folks. Both very serious things. I want to do something that is more fun."

He was seeing a new Rose. "Such as?"

"Can't you take a bit of initiative, Peter?"

At this point the bus arrived and they got on. Conditions on the crowded bus did not make for good conversation. It is hard to open your mouth to talk when you might end up with a mouthful of a stranger's hair.

It was not until they got off, therefore, that the conversation resumed. "There's a good noodle shop just down the road," Peter said. "We could have a snack together."

"Yes, that does sound a little better. Unless we have any other pastoral visits to do."

"I'm sorry," Peter said. "No, this will be just the two of us."

"Good!"

They found the shop and Peter made the order. As they waited for delivery, Rose's hand extended across the table and he seized it. They smiled. "That's more like it," she said.

It was not a brilliant meal, but it served its purpose. Peter went on, "I would like us to become good friends. In a way it is just as if I never knew you before."

"Yes, I would like us to become friends. "

"It could even lead to marriage." He became a bit embarrassed. "That wasn't a proposal, but it could turn into one. I'm beginning to feel – well---"

"Go on."

"A sort of love for you."

"I was wondering when you would start using that word. Yes, I suppose I could say the same."

The arrival of the noodles they had ordered broke into their conversation. It was also the signal to unlock their hands.

"Why don't you come to my place for an evening meal tomorrow?" Rose suggested.

"That would be lovely. Don't go to a lot of trouble."

"Why not? You're worth it."

"We could have plenty of opportunity for talking – and maybe other things."

The idea of 'other things' excited him. Yes, a new chapter had begun for both of them.

68

After another busy day at the shop, Arnold was glad to get back to his family. They had their usual meal together, and the bedtime rituals followed. After this they always enjoyed a cup of coffee and the opportunity to chat.

"Have you been anywhere interesting today?" he asked.

"Not really."

"You didn't take Sammy out anywhere?"

"No. We just stayed at home."

Arnold was concerned about this. He had been intending to talk with Kathleen about this topic for some time. "This has something to do with the accident, hasn't it?"

"Yes, I suppose it has."

"You haven't taken Sammy out much lately, have you?"

"No, I haven't. He doesn't complain. He seems perfectly happy at home."

"But it isn't natural for him to stay at home all the time. You know that what happened was a one-off thing. It is highly unlikely it would happen again – especially if we are careful and protect him."

"I know, but I can't help it. I feel scared. I keep seeing him as he was on that day."

"You've got to get over it. That is in the past. We still have our lives to live."

"I know; but I can't shake it off. I'm sorry to be like this, but it isn't my choice."

Supposing I take a bit more time off work and we take him out together?"

"I don't want to stop you doing your job."

"I would be happy to do that. How would you feel about it?"

Suddenly she burst into tears. He went and sat next to her and put his arm round her. "I'm sorry," she said at last. Then after some more heaving she went on, "Do we have to stay here?"

"We're going to have our furlough soon, as you well know. That should help you get back to normal."

"But do we have to come back? You've often said you would like to get back into journalism. Maybe that's what you're meant to do."

"I came here because I felt God was calling me here, and I thought it was the same for you."

"It was, but things change. We've had some good times, but I feel we ought to think seriously about staying home."

"You would never have said that before Sammy's accident."

"Maybe that had to happen to persuade us to move on."

"I'm sorry, my love, but I don't see it that way."

"But you would love to be back in journalism. You're wasted here."

"I wouldn't say that."

"Give it some thought. Not just for my sake and Sammy's sake, but your own."

"I must confess that I had wondered."

"There we are. So you had actually considered staying in the UK."

"Not so seriously."

"But maybe you should."

"I would need guidance."

"Isn't this enough to get you started?"

"Let me think and pray more about it. We've both got to be prepared to stay on if that is what God wants."

"Sometimes he guides us through circumstances. Look, Arnold, I don't want to be a drag. All I ask is that we both look at this situation seriously. I think you would still be young enough to get back into the work you love. But if you wait too long---"

"Who says I don't love the work I'm, doing here?"

"I'm your wife. I can tell that you're not entirely satisfied with it."

"All right. I'll pray for guidance. Does that satisfy you?"

"Don't be angry. Try and respect how I feel."

He hugged her more tightly. It was still hard to understand how she could have changed so much in just a short time.

69

When Rose got back to the seminary she found an unexpected visitor waiting outside her door. It was Catherine, and her eyes lit up when she saw her missionary friend. . "I've been waiting for you," she explained.

"This is a pleasant surprise," Rose said. "Do come in."

They went inside and Rose put the kettle on. "It's such a long time since we met," she said. "Are you married now? We have not had any news for a long time."

"No, I'm sorry about that. I was supposed to be married by now."

"Supposed to? You mean, it hasn't happened yet?"

"It has all changed. You know how they do things round here. The two of us had never met. It was arranged for us to meet at his parents' house. So that is where we met up for the first time."

"And what did you think of him?"

"It was not easy to know in that sort of situation; but I was not attracted to him. He did not seem very cheerful or friendly. I sensed he was there only because his parents said he had to be – rather like myself really."

"Tea or coffee?"

"Tea, please. No sugar."

"That is how it always used to be. It was all arranged for you and you just had to learn to like the other person. That is all changing now. People can marry anyone they like. But there are still a lot of parents who prefer the old ways, and that is what our parents are like."

"And when is the marriage supposed to take place?"

"That's just it. It isn't going to take place."

"Praise the Lord! How come?"

"Well, it seems that my fiancé had another girl friend, and that he was very much in love with her. Our parents did not know about this. At first he agreed to what his parents said; but after that meeting he knew it was wrong. At least, that is what I think it must have been like. He suddenly told his parents that he was going to marry this other girl, and that if they tried to stop him he would run away."

"How did they take it?"

"They were shocked. You know how we Chinese have a lot of respect for our parents. They thought he was being disloyal and they were very angry; but he stood up to them and would not budge."

"So what is the situation now?"

"It looks as if our wedding is off. His parents have been trying hard to persuade him to change his mind."

"And what about your own father?"

"He can't understand. He only knows the traditional ways. But if the marriage is off, he knows he can no longer force me into marriage. He is very disappointed, but I don't think he is so keen to marry me off to anybody else in case it all goes wrong again."

"How do you feel? You must be very relieved."

"Yes, I feel so glad. I didn't want to marry him."

"What about your studies? Will you come back?"

"I would like to. It is too early to say."

"You would have to start the year again."

"I know."

"One of your teachers would be different."

"Oh? Which one?"

"Sz Lausu. She is going back to the USA."

"Really? I don't know what to say." She looked thoughtful. "She is a good teacher, but I'm a bit afraid of her."

"I hope you will be able to come back here and resume your course."

"I hope so too."

After a little time together, Rose walked with her to the gate. On the way back she met up with Bill Smythe, who also taught there. He seemed perplexed.

"Have you seen anything of Frank?" he asked.

"No. I usually deal with the female students. I don't know the men very well. Is there a problem?"

"He was supposed to come to see me this morning but he didn't show up. I went to ask his dorm mates but they had not seen him. It isn't like him."

"There is probably a simple explanation."

"Yes, let's hope so."

70

Alleyne was just returning from a walk with Sandy. They had visited a park, where she was able to let him have a run off the lead. He had been running around like a mad thing, but when it was time to return to his mistress, he did so obediently. She felt so proud of him, that he had such absolute loyalty to her; but it still pained her that they would soon have to separate. How on earth was she going to find anyone who would care for him as much as she had done?

As she approached the seminary gate, someone was just coming out. It was Ke-lin. She looked hard, just in case she had been mistaken. No mistake at all. "Why, it's Ke-lin," she declared, trying to sound as friendly as she could. Sandy did not seem to mind stopping, as it would prolong the excursion

"Sz Lausu! I just came on a visit."

"We have missed you. Are you married yet?"

A man was cleaning his teeth and spitting into the gutter. A funny time of day to be doing it. "No," the girl said, "I am not married"; then she told Alleyne the same story that she had told Rose.

"I'm so pleased for you," Alleyne responded. "Does this mean you will be coming back to college?"

"I hope so. It hasn't been decided yet."

"That would be in September, I suppose."

"Yes. I would have to do the same year all over again."

"That would be good for you, as you missed so much when your mother was ill."

"I was just talking with Li Lausu. She told me you would be leaving the college."

This was like a dagger at her throat. They were getting rid of her already. "I will be very sad to leave," she admitted, "but my mission has other important work for me to do. It needs a person with a lot of experience, so they have offered the job to me."

"I am glad to hear it. Not glad that you are going, but glad you will have a good job."

Soon after that they parted company. On the surface it had been a friendly encounter; but she could not help feeling that Ke-lin had been somewhat guarded in her attitude. Maybe she still held it against her that she had criticized her work.

She took out her key, opened the door, and filled a bowl with water for the dog, as he was panting heavily. Yes, perhaps she was a hard taskmaster – or should it be taskmistress?-- at times, but it was because she wanted to get the best out of people. Surely it was not wrong to be a little strict in the interests of progress. That sort of thing did not make her popular, but that was not what she was here for. Over the years, people had come to appreciate her work, even though they did not always find it easy to like her.

Sometimes matters did not work out as she would have wished. She recalled that fellow Liu who had worked in the office ten years earlier and been caught stealing. At the time she had thought that exposing him would make him more careful about his honesty in the future. Sadly, it had not worked that way. Word had reached her from time to time of further acts of dishonesty which had brought him into conflict with the police. It was hard to change some people. It was two or three years since she had heard anything of him. Maybe he had moved to another part of the country. She would probably never see or hear of him again.

Sandy looked up at her with his tail wagging as if to ask whether it was time for the next meal.

71

The next morning, having returned from a time of prayer with James Yang at the Good Shepherd rectory, Peter was in the study completing his preparations for Sunday's sermon.

Suddenly he noticed that Paul was walking past. Immediately he leaped to the door, opened it and called out, "How's Jenny?"

Paul turned on his heel, came up the steps and sat down with him in the room. "She's making good progress," he said. "She will be in hospital for a while, but the leg should heal nicely."

"I'm so glad."

"I have another friend. The same thing happened to him, but his girl died. The police treated him as a criminal. It was very hard for him."

"I'm sorry to hear that."

"Jenny's parents are very kind."

"How do you mean?"

"There is a law here. If you are hurt in an accident you can claim a lot of money for compensation. Some people exaggerate their injuries in order to get more money."

"Yes, I can picture that. I had a friend who was driving a car. There was a man on a bicycle in front of him wobbling from side to side. When he slightly scraped the bicycle and the man fell off, he seemed to be ok; but when he saw it was a foreigner in a car he pretended to be badly injured in order to get more money."

"Yes, that sort of thing does happen. But Jenny's parents are not claiming anything against me, despite the hospital fees. I am very fortunate."

"After all, you said the accident was not your fault."

"That is true, yet I still feel bad about it."

"Just be thankful that she is still alive."

"Yes, God preserved her life."

"And now you were obviously going somewhere and I mustn't hold you up."

"Thanks, pastor."

Peter returned to his preparations. After a few minutes, however, he noticed Simon coming in the opposite direction. He must be returning from his home village. Simon came up the the door, and asked to come in.

It was Simon who opened this second conversation.

"Remember what I said yesterday?"

"We talked about a lot of things."

"I said they did not know I was a Christian."

"Yes, I remember that."

"Well, after you had gone, they asked me a lot of questions. In the end I had to admit that I was now a Christian. My father got very angry and he began to beat me with a stick."

"Really? He did not look like that kind of person."

"He's a very strong follower of traditional religions. He accused me of going against the religion and tradition of my family. He's still angry this morning."

"What are you going to do about it?"

"He will calm down. I know my father. He will gradually accept the change, but it will not be easy. I think that if you went back there at the moment they would not give you such warm hospitality."

"They were very kind to us when we was there."

"Yes, they are very kind at heart, but they are only comfortable with the things they have grown up with. They don't like change. All this will take time."

"You think they will come to accept it?"

"After a while. I know my parents."

After this second conversation, Peter resumed his work. It was hard to concentrate. He was thinking about both conversations. He was also thinking about going to Rose's place in the evening for a meal. It would be the first time they had been alone together, and he was looking forward to it so much. They would kiss and there would be some hugging. How quickly things were changing between them. How could he have been so slow to admit how he felt about her?

72

It was a quiet Saturday morning at the shop, with the ceiling fan whirring against the summer heat, when Pastor Fan came in. He asked for a book, which Arnold was more than happy to supply. As he paid for it, he announced, "We are already making plans for next year."

"Plans for what?"

"Our annual evangelistic meetings. There is a Chinese born in Indonesia who is making a big impression. We have just booked him and he is looking forward to his visit. I trust you will be able to bring some books."

"If I am here. We am going on furlough soon and it is not clear what happens after that."

At this point Pastor Fan frowned. "Yes, I should have thought about that." Arnold was not clear what he meant by this, but a further explanation was forthcoming. Fortunately, Pastor Fan's Mandarin was normally very clear, and he did not have much problem understanding what he said. "You have a helper, a young man from the seminary."

"That's right. Frank is a great help to me when we go out to the villages. He is very good at befriending people."

"I'm glad to hear it. But have you heard the latest news?"

"No. What is that?"

"He has disappeared."

"What do you mean – disappeared?"

"As you know, he lives in a dormitory at the seminary. At this time of the year there are plenty of comings and goings. Students who live not far away like to go home to be with their parents. Two days ago this Frank, as you call him, took a walk out of the seminary gates and was not seen again. His parents say that he has not been home either."

"Maybe he is staying with a friend."

"Maybe so, but I doubt it. There are reports – unconfirmed, of course – that he was seen getting into a car."

"How do you know all this?"

"I make it my business as a pastor to know everything that goes on in this town. How well do you know him?"

"He has been helping me only for a short time."

"And are you aware of his political views?"

"Yes, he does share them with me from time to time."

"You know, then, that he is a member of a group that is seeking independence for Taiwan."

"I thought Taiwan was already independent."

"Yes, but he is opposed to the Kwomintang. He wants rulers who do not belong to that party. Did he say anything about that to you?"

"Yes, he said something a few days ago. I thought it was a bit extreme."

"In Taiwan today those are dangerous views to be held. You are in danger of being arrested by the Secret Police."

"I thought that only happened in Mainland China."

"It happens here too – for different reasons."

"And what will happen to him now, if this is true?"

"Who knows? We may never hear anything more of him again."

"But this is supposed to be Free China".

"Free as long as you keep to the rules. Frank was outside the rules."

"I found him a very friendly young man. I would hate to think that anything terrible would happen to him."

"I fully agree. But we don't make the laws which control this country. I know it is hard for you to accept this, but I thought it my duty to tell you."

"How do you know all this?"

"I have friends...."

"Is there any way we can help him?"

"Not without coming under suspicion. In fact, the government will probably be keeping a keen eye on you."

"On me? What have I done?"

"You are a friend of this young man. He has shared his ideas with you. For all they know, you are in agreement with him."

"I must admit that what he said sounded convincing."

"I thought I ought to warn you. They will not make it obvious. But they will be there."

"Thanks. But I'm not sure where that leaves me."

"You must be careful not to speak of those views with anyone else. Pretend that you have heard nothing."

"Have I got black marks against my name?"

"I expect so. I don't think they will go so far as to arrest you."

"Then what will they do?"

"You said you would be going home on furlough soon."

"Yes, I did."

"Then when you apply to come back they may refuse you a visa."

"Simply because I knew Frank?"

"Yes. Their intelligence services are very thorough. There is, of course, no guarantee that this would happen, but I think that it is likely. You need to know this if you are making plans for the future."

"I appreciate your telling me all this; but I still don't understand how you know so much about the situation."

"I have my sources. I'm sorry if what I say has been a disappointment to you. I for one have valued your friendship and your work here in the shop and I would be sorry to see you go."

It was as if his work here was already in the past. Maybe this would be a strong contributory factor to their planning for the next step.

"Well, I have a to go and see someone in hospital," Pastor Fan declared. "I hope I haven't disturbed you too much". With these words he swept out of the shop, leaving Arnold with much to think about.

73

Rose was at the market to buy food for the meal which she was going to cook for Peter and herself. Owing to the primitive conditions, she could not produce gourmet food, but she still wanted to do her best. As she entered the market the flower ladies did their best as usual to attract her attention, but she simply smiled and walked on.

Her first thought was for meat. As there was no refrigeration in the market, it was usually wise to buy meat on the day of consumption. Although she had not asked Peter about his preferences, she thought a small joint of pork would be acceptable. The woman who served her tried to persuade her to buy a much bigger joint than she had in mind but was, after some argument, open to reason. When buying vegetables she also had to resist the attempts to make her spend more than she had planned. Even so, the whole meal would cost much less than it would have done at an English market.

It was not that she was trying to impress Peter. That was not what it was all about. The main thing was that they would be able to enjoy one another's company. Of course, it would be good to show him that she knew how to cook, as that would be important if they should decide to marry, but she did not have to prove anything. Just being together was the main object of setting this up.

She had much to think about as she walked back. Once again she recalled Miss Price's words that many female missionaries would remain single. For a long time she had lived with an acceptance of the likelihood that this would be her fate. Now it looked as if all this might change.

She thought of the friends who had travelled out with her on the ship. Betty, like herself, had remained single, and was heavily involved in clinic evangelism. Letty had died of food poisoning through eating cold meat at a wedding. Fiona had married a fellow missionary and already had two children, a boy and a girl. How much their paths had diverged! God had a particular plan for each one, and it was right to agree with his plan and to follow it through without complaint.

The main thing now was that both Peter and herself should understand God's plan in relation to their friendship. It still amazed her how quickly the relationship had come alive in the past few days. Having got as far as this she now understood how much of a tactile person she was. She needed to embrace and be embraced. After the meal they would have some opportunity to explore. Of course, being Christians, they would be aware of their limits. Nevertheless she was really looking forward to Peter's touch.

Marriage was not just two minds thinking alike. It was also a sexual thing. That was how God had ordained it. In committing themselves to one another, they would be expressing this in a full sexual relationship, but only after marriage. She deplored the changing mores in Western society. Things which would never have been conceived of in the past had now become common practice. She was not a prig, but she still wanted to honour the Lord in this relationship, if it should develop.

A young couple holding hands walked past in the opposite direction. Even that was frowned upon by many in Chinese society unless a couple had become engaged. It would be hard for Peter and herself to develop their relationship without exciting local interest.. It was a bit like love in a goldfish bowl.

Whether they met at her place or his they were under the eye of observant students.

Was she reading too much into the situation? She had to admit that, if their relationship came to nothing, she would be greatly disappointed; but somehow she thought that would not be the case. Maybe one day she would be able to introduce Miss Price to her husband.

74

Alleyne Zimmer could not set her mind at rest until the mystery of Helen's death was solved. On this Saturday morning she went again to the college library to see if there was anything about it in the newspaper. Although she had known Chinese all her life, it was still a bit of a struggle to make sense of newspaper articles because of journalistic quirks, but she was determined to keep up with the news.

Just as she was opening the 'paper and her eyes had lighted on a piece of news that could be what she was looking for, the principal, Timothy Lee, who had been examining some books in another part of the library, noticed her and came up to speak.

"It is very creditable that an American woman such as yourself can read Chinese newspapers."

"Don't forget," she said, looking up, "that I have been living in a Chinese culture almost all my life. Longer than you have," she added.

"Yes, you are one of us," he declared with a rare twinkle.

"And I like to know what is happening around me."

"You have shown a lot of interest in the matter of your friend's murder."

"Of course. She was a good friend, and the whole thing is very tragic. I think there is something about it here."

"There is. Would you care to come to my office, and we can talk about it? Here we may disturb other people."

"Very well." She got up and followed the principal to his room. When the door was closed, he sat at his desk with his hands clenched together and said, "We can talk here more freely."

"I thought there was an article about it in this morning's newspaper," she said. "I was just going to read it."

"Yes, that is what I want to talk with you about. Apparently they have done some fingerprinting and the prints matched those of a young man who is already in their records."

"And what is his name? I had not quite got as far as reading that."

"His name is Liu."

"That is quite a common name. Is that all it says?"

"No, there is more. But what concerns me is that he was once connected with this college."

Nothing could have prepared her for that. It was as if someone had just punched her below the belt.

"You don't mean the man who used to work in the office here?"

"The same." He paused, while he allowed his words to sink in. Then he went on, "I believe you knew him."

"I didn't know him very well. He was caught stealing money. That was something that had to be dealt with."

"This was before my time, but I hear that you were the one who decided to call the police."

"It seemed the right thing to do. If he was brought before the police in this instance, I thought that it would make him think twice about re-offending."

"But it did not work out that way, did it? The man has been in trouble with the police on several other occasions."

"It must be in his nature. Some people are like that." Although she did not show it, she wondered whether her own harsh treatment of the man had encouraged him to pursue a life of crime rather than dissuading him from it."

"It is unfortunate," the principal went on, "that the college should be implicated in this matter. I suggest that we say as little about it as we can. We don't want to tarnish the college's reputation."

"Does it say any more about him? His motive, for instance?"

"Burglary, of course. A large sum of money was found at his place, and he could not explain where it had come from. Probably the result of several burglaries. Did your friend keep a lot of money in the house?"

"Yes. I told her that it was unwise, but she would not listen to me."

"Unfortunately there are some people who do not trust our banks. I don't know how this Mr. Liu knew about it or whether he was just taking a chance."

"I don't suppose we shall ever know that. Helen certainly didn't boast about having money in the house – though she did tell me as a friend she could trust."

"This cook – he must have surprised the man, and was stabbed before he could do anything about it. You have heard that his body, weighted with stones, was thrown into a sort of pond just outside the house?"

"Yes, I misjudged the man. At first I thought he was the one who had done it."

"And it is obvious that the killer wanted other people to think that way as well."

"And your friend must have seen him do it, and she had to be silenced as well."

"It is just like the sort of thing you would read about in a cheap novel. Not that I read such things."

"Things like this happen in real life as well."

"It came as a big shock to me."

"I know it did and I am concerned for you. What I would ask of you is that you try to keep the college's name out of this. It would not be good for us if we got dragged into this news story."

Was that all he wanted? For her it was a personal tragedy; for him it was just a matter that could affect the reputation of the college. However, she was not going to talk about it with anyone, for she did not wish to be reminded of the harsh way she had dealt with the original matter.

"I have no intention of talking about it," she responded.

"I am glad to hear it," the principal replied. "The man is an incorrigible criminal and this sort of thing would have happened even if he had not at one time been connected with us." He went on: "Now that the man has been caught, this matter is over. He will be tried, will receive the death penalty and we can put this whole thing behind us."

It was one thing to say that, but the whole matter was burned deeply into her mind. If she had been more lenient ten years ago would this man have been stopped in his tracks? In a sense, she could be held responsible for the death of her friend, as her own attitude to the man could have sent him into decline. Although she still believed she had acted rightly at the time, she still had nagging doubts. Now she wanted to get away from the principal, to get away from everyone and think about this whole tragic affair in the silence of her own company.

75

The next morning, as Peter prepared for the service, he could not help thinking of his experience of the previous evening. The meal had been simple, for the conditions were very restricted. One could not produce a gourmet meal on one small double burner. But Rose had done her best under such restrictions.

As for what followed.... He smiled with pleasure. It was as if he had hardly known her before. In their kisses and their embraces they were like two hungry people permitted for the first time to enjoy good food. He could hardly believed that their relationship had changed so much in such a short time. But it was not just the physical contact: it was the deep emotion that went with it. Both of them were conscious of a love which had so far evaded them in all their years of adulthood. Now that it had come to the fore, there was no going back. For the first time in his life he felt really complete. There had been girl friends before, of whom the chief had been Cynthia, but they had never raised him to such heights. Although they were not yet pledged to marry, he could not see how this relationship could turn out any other way.

Rose had told him that, instead of going to her usual church, she would join his congregation this morning. That might turn a few heads! She had attended once with Cynthia, but that was different.

As he stood at the door to welcome people, the Bakkers were the first to arrive, closely followed by the Smythes. Two of the students, Mark and Simon, slipped in. Then she came. She was wearing a pale green floral dress that he had not seen before. As he greeted her, his heart missed a beat. Yes, something very special was happening. The Smythes turned to look at her with some surprise: probably they had not guessed that there was any sort of relationship between them. Last of all came the Eastwickers, with a scowling Craig in tow.

Peter found that he wanted to conduct the service well to give Rose a good impression. Immediately he corrected himself. Surely his aim was to honour the Lord and in so doing to meet the needs of these worshippers. Yet he still found that he wanted Rose to see that he was good at his job.

It was very different from those services in Manchester, yet he enjoyed the intimacy of this small group. Whether there was a large congregation or just a handful, God had promised that his presence would be with them. In such a situation there was no room for anonymity.

As the service progressed the ceiling fan was whirring at maximum speed in order to counter the oppressive heat and humidity. Even so, Rick Bakker, who was heavily built, would take out a handkerchief every so often to mop his fevered brow. In his home conditions, no doubt he would use air conditioning most of the time in the summer. Coming to such a church as this represented some personal sacrifice.

At the close of the service, they all had coffee. Vickie came up to Peter and asked, "This is your friend?"
"This is Rose," he replied. "She works at the seminary."
Vickie shook hands with her. "You two good friends?" she asked.

"Yes, we are actually," Rose replied.

"I can see that," Vicky replied. "I think I like you better than Cynthia, though she had her good points."

"She was class," Craig suggested.

"You must come and have a meal with us sometime, both of you," Vickie suggested.

"Thanks," Rose replied. "I would enjoy that."

The Smythes confirmed his thinking. "We didn't know you were friends, but we are very glad to see it. We think you are well suited."

The biscuits (or cookies, as they would say) had been provided by the Bakkers. These did not last long, as Mark was very fond of American products, especially when they were edible. At last, the other worshippers had gone, and Peter and Rose were left alone.

"You did very well," she said. "I'm glad I came."

"I'm glad too," he said.

"Not a very big congregation but very friendly."

"I like to think so."

"I won't come here regularly," she said. "I'm too involved with my local church."

"I didn't expect you to."

"Of course, it would be different if---" She stopped herself.

"I know just what you mean. Early days yet."

"Now I have an invitation to lunch. See you tonight at the meeting?"

"Yes, I'll call round at the usual time."

"That is good then."

76

Sunday lunch was over, the boys were playing together, and Arnold and Kathleen relaxed in a shady spot on their recliners and chatted together. He had already told her about his conversation with Pastor Fan.

"It really looks as if we're being led back home," she

commented.

"Afraid so," he replied.

"But you've never been really satisfied with the job at the bookshop, have you?"

"It had its good points. I enjoyed the village trips."

"But you're a journalist at heart."

"I suppose I am and always will be."

"Not that I ever knew you in those days; but I can see it from things you've said."

"What would you do if we went back?"

"Concentrate on being a good mum, and then see if something else turns up."

"Like what?"

"I don't know. I was a secretary once, but you know that."

"It could be difficult, sure it could, getting back into journalism after being away so long."

"But you haven't lost your touch. I think they would welcome you."

"It's hard to say. If I had stayed on, I might even have been an editor by now; but it would be almost like starting at the beginning again."

"I don't think that will worry you."

"It's hard to get used to the prospect of not coming back. I thought I would be here most of my life, sure I did."

"But we would have to think of the boys' education. They could get a good American education here, but how would that prepare them for British universities?"

"Yes, there is that consideration as well."

"It is important we do what is right for them."

"I know. There's a lot to think about."

"But you can't really see us coming back, can you?"

"I don't think so." He was still adjusting to all this. "The Sunday evening group would miss us."

"They can meet somewhere else. Ours isn't the only home."

"But they seemed to like it here. They will be sorry to hear we are going."

"You said 'will', not 'would'."

"Yes, I suppose it's inevitable."

"But if we are to go home next month. there is one thing I would like to do."

"What's that?"

"Go back to Sun Moon Lake. Just for a visit, I mean."

"No problem. I was thinking of going somewhere."

"You know why, don't you?"

"Because we first met there?"

"Right first time. I will always treasure that place, since it brought us together."

"We seemed so young then, sure we were."

"It wasn't all that long ago."

"I know. What is it? Ten years?"

"Exactly."

"The boys should enjoy another visit there."

"They enjoy any excuse for a holiday."

"You remember last time, when Philip's leg was grabbed by a monkey?"

"Yes, it really scared him for a while. He should not have gone so near to it."

"You're not afraid to go again?"

"You don't see many monkeys on tethers. And, anyway, they are not as dangerous as drainage gutters."

"You will never forget that, will you?"

"I can't get it out of my mind. I want my sons to grow up in a safe environment."

"There is no environment that is perfectly safe, sure there isn't. Especially if you live in Northern Ireland."

"We don't have to live over there, do we? After all, I don't come from there. Things seem particularly bad at the moment. We could stay at my mum's near London until we find a place for ourselves."

"We are going to need to do a lot of talking about this. It's not all bad in Northern Ireland. Some areas are perfectly safe, sure they are."

"That's what people say; but is there really anywhere that is safe? 'Safe' just means that nobody has set off a bomb yet in that area."

"We always used to talk about the Lord's leading. Can't we expect him to lead us this time to the right place, whether in the London area, in Northern Ireland or elsewhere?"

"I haven't forgotten that. No, we must look to the Lord's leading, wherever we go."

"And the boys will feel at home anywhere, as long as we're with them."

Arnold closed his eyes. Yes, despite the disruption of what they had regarded as their normal life, he was beginning to feel relaxed again.

77

When they met to go to the evening meeting, Rose was still wearing the floral dress, for she had observed how much Peter admired it. It was not a very convenient costume for cycling, but she would ride with care. It was strange to reflect that this was the first time they had met with the others in the short period since this relationship between them had sprung to life: it seemed as if it was much longer than that.

They did not talk much during the journey: being together was enough. When they got there, Kathleen opened the door to them. "Won't be a moment," she whispered. "Just finishing off the bedtime story."

"We can answer the door for you," Rose assured her. Just a few moments after she had said it, the bell rang. It was Big Lil.

"Had a great meeting last night," she exclaimed before Rose had even had opportunity to ask her anything. "You should've seen them demons: they couldn't get away fast enough." She said this as if this were normal practice for everyone. "You could feel the power of the Lord so real."

"Glad to hear it," Rose replied, conscious that it was a very inadequate response to such mighty dealings.

The next to arrive was Tim Holloran. "Guess I'm not the first one today," he exclaimed as he walked in and saw the others. "Had a bit of a holdup on the way."

"Yes, you're usually a bit earlier than this," Peter remarked.

"Anybody heard about that guy from the seminary who disappeared?" Tim asked.

"I haven't heard anything," Rose replied. "We are getting very concerned."

"You knew that he was involved with Arnold in taking the van round the villages, didn't you?" Peter interjected.

At that moment Arnold himself came in, and Kathleen went to put the kettle on. "You're talking about Frank?" he queried.

"Yes", Tim went on. Nobody seems to know what happened to the guy. Have you heard?"

Arnold seemed to be pondering what to say. "No definite news of him," he said at last.

"Maybe he has a problem and needs deliverance," Big Lil suggested, but nobody took this seriously.

It was at this point that Sister Cecilia arrived. "I'm sorry to be late," she remarked when she saw that the room was already full.

"You're not late," Arnold assured her. "We are just having refreshments, and the meeting will start in a little while."

Rose warmed to all these friends. She would miss them when she went on furlough; but, hopefully, when she returned, she would be able to enjoy this fellowship again.

Tim, always one for the latest news, observed, "They caught the man who murdered that teacher."

This embarrassed Rose. The staff at the seminary had been encouraged not to speak of this matter, since the prisoner had once worked at the school. "He has not been put on trial yet," she remarked.

"But it's pretty obvious, isn't it?"

"I feel sorry for Miss Zimmer," Rose went on. "That was the one friend she had. Although she won't admit it, you can see by her face that she is devastated."

"I can imagine it," said Kathleen as she came in with the tea and coffee. The poor woman doesn't make friends very easily. It must have been a big blow."

"But she doesn't admit it," Rose said. "She doesn't want to talk to anybody about it."

"A pity she doesn't belong to this group," Sister Cecilia said. "I have always found I could bring my problems here and get the help I need."

"Some people don't find it easy to wear their heart on their sleeve," Peter suggested. "She is a very private person."

"Yes, I have never really got to know her," Arnold admitted.

"She needs ministry," Big Lil declared. "She can't handle this on her own."

"We can't do anything," Arnold suggested, "unless she asks for it. Hasn't she spoken to <u>you</u> ?" He faced Rose with the question.

"She is not that sort of person," Rose replied. She believes it is a sign of weakness to confide in other people."

Just then the doorbell rang.

78

It was one thing on top of another. Alleyne had never been one to panic in the midst of a crisis. She knew that she had within herself an innate strength which enabled her to cope without outside help no matter how severe the circumstances. It was a special quality which God had give her.

She had imagined then that she would still be able to cope despite what she was going through. It had been a terrible blow when her one good friend had been cruelly murdered. On top of this came the news that she would apparently be leaving Taiwan for good. Just as she was learning to carry these two burdens, she had discovered that the murderer was a man whose path of crime could have stemmed from her own unforgiving spirit. Even though she had felt at the time she had made the right decision, nagging doubts now assailed her. Every so often she felt tears welling up within her, and she sought to get alone so as not to have to admit to anyone else that she could not handle the situation. She prayed a lot about it. God would give her strength. But the tears persisted. She was afraid to face others, lest she should break down in front of them and all she had stood for over the years be ruined.

That Sunday she had kept away from church, as she had no wish to betray her feelings. By evening, however, she felt desperately alone. What was she going to do? One thought flashed into her mind. Rose had often invited her to join the prayer group. From the start she had dismissed the whole idea. She did not need others. That was not the way she functioned. But at the moment she was not functioning anyway.

Eventually she decided to take a walk. She would take back alleyways, where nobody would know her. If she happened to find herself near the place where they met for prayer, she might just go to join them. Probably she would not; but the possibility was there.

When Sandy saw that she was going out, his tail began to wag.

"No, not this time, Sandy. You've had three walks today. This one is different."

Soon she was out in the alleyways, walking almost aimlessly. Her mind was tormented with the problems that were plaguing her. There was also the problem of finding a home for Sandy when she left. Her whole world was crumbling.

After a while she looked about her. Yes, this was the area where the Maguires lived. Rose had given her the number and she was standing just outside the place. Had God led her here for a purpose? Hesitantly she stretched out a finger. There was the sound of a bell. The decision was made.

It was Kathleen who opened the door. Immediately she recognised Alleyne and invited her in. They were all gathered there. There was an air of pleasure and surprise as they saw her. She knew that she was welcomed. A young fellow got up from his chair and invited her to sit there. She accepted.

"It's so good to see you," Rose said, and it was obvious that she meant it.

Alleyne was about to answer, but the words would not come. Instead, she burst into uncontrollable tears. She felt acutely embarrassed, but she could not help herself. Rose knelt beside her and took her hand. Kathleen also knelt there and took the other hand. A big, corpulent woman whom she did not know started praying in a foreign language, which was a bit unsettling. They continued like this for some time. Nobody said anything to her. She liked that. They were ready to share her grief without trying to solve anything. She had never been in this position before and she felt a kind of warmth inside.

This continued for a long time. At the end of this time she found her tears stopped flowing.

"Feel better?" Rose smiled.

"Yes, I sure do." They were the first words she had uttered.

The young man who had given her his seat, said, "My name's Tim. I'm from the States too."

"It was kind of you to give me your seat. Of course, I'm really from China. The American bit is incidental. It's almost a foreign country to me."

"Yes, you're really old school," Tim went on to say.

"Can I get you some coffee?" Kathleen asked.

"A glass of water would be enough."

"You don't have to say anything if you don't want to," Peter said. "We all understand your situation."

"I thought I was strong enough to handle this," Alleyne said, sniffing, "but I guess I was wrong."

Kathleen handed her a glass of water, and she sipped it tentatively.

The big woman said, "If you would like us to lay hands on you we could---"

Rose replied quickly. "I don't think that that is something Miss Zimmer would want."

Alleyne squeezed her hand. How Rose understood her.

"I feel I'm interrupting," Alleyne said suddenly.

"No," Arnold replied. "That's what we're here for."

"Were you doing anything important when I arrived?"

"We're doing something important now," Arnold said. It was obvious that he meant it.

"I thought I could handle all this. I was doing well, but this last thing was too much for me."

"What thing was that?" Arnold asked.

"I discovered that I had met the man who killed her. It was a long time ago. I was very judgmental. Might have set him off the rails."

"Don't blame yourself," said Rose.

"I don't think I should talk about it."

Arnold assured her, "You're free to say anything you want here – or just to keep quiet."

"Thanks." She gave a sniff and changed the subject.. "I can't keep worrying about my little dog, Sandy. What happens to him when I go?"

"Miss Zimmer is going back to the States," Arnold explained, in case anyone did not know.

For the first time an oriental woman in a nun's habit spoke. "We just lost our little dog."

"That's Sister Cecilia," Kathleen explained. "She lives at a convent."

"I didn't know they had dogs in a convent," Alleyne said.

"We do," said Sister Cecilia.

"Sounds like a good idea," Alleyne exclaimed.

"We would love to get a new dog. Do you think your dog would like to live with us?"

"As long as he gets his walks. He is very well behaved."

"I'm sure he is. You must have trained him well."

"I would need to tell you all about him."

"Of course. We want get to know him properly. Maybe you would like to come over to the convent and see things for yourself."

The very idea of going to a Roman Catholic institution would have been anathema, but she found herself saying, "Yes, I would like to see where he could be going."

"We can arrange that. It will be good to have a visitors."

"That's a load off my mind. I want him to go where he will be loved and well treated."

"Of course. We will look after him well."

Alleyne looked round her. "Please carry on. I'm fine now. Do what you normally do."

"We normally do a lot of praying," Arnold said. "And since you have come here to share with us, would you like us to pray with you? Just gently, of course, no laying on of hands unless you request it."

"Yes, I would like that."

79

Peter could not help admiring the way in which Rose was relating to Alleyne Zimmer. The woman was hard to get to know and she had never treated Rose very well, yet Rose was demonstrating a deep concern for her. All this made him admire her all the more. When they were praying for their unexpected visitor, Rose was at the forefront of the praying, since she knew her better than anyone else did, and he could tell that the prayers were heartfelt.

When the prayers were ended, the older woman sat back with tears in her eyes and said a simply 'thank you'.

"We haven't done any singing yet," Arnold declared. "How

about 'Burdens Are Lifted at Calvary'?"

It was a good choice, for it was traditional enough for Miss Zimmer to know and like it, and she even joined in the singing. When the song was over, Arnold asked, "Is there anyone else who has special needs at this time?" Tim told them about a young lecturer whom he was getting to know and requested prayer for his salvation; so they spent some time praying for him. Sister Cecilia spoke of a newly arrived American nun who was having difficulty settling in, so they also prayed about this.

Arnold then turned to Peter. "Have you any special needs, Peter?" The question took him by surprise. He stole a glance at Rose, and, sensing a reason for this, she gave a little nod. So he began: "I'm not sure how to put this. It isn't something we would go public about right now; but you may have noticed that Rose and I are becoming very good friends. These are early days yet, but we are both wondering whether God wants us to be together long-term."

"Do you love each other?" Big Lil demanded.

"Why, yes."

"Then what's to stop you?"

"I must say," said Tim, "that I could see that you two were getting closer. I'm surprised it didn't happen before."

Things were going too fast for Peter. "We're not engaged or anything," he said. "We're still trying to work out what is right."

"It certainly worked for Arnold and me," Kathleen put in; "but, then, with us it was love at first sight."

"Each of us has to look for the way that is best for us," Arnold stated. "We don't want to embarrass you both, and we won't make any assumptions; but if you want the humble opinion of a friend, I think you were made for each other. Do you want us to pray for you both?"

"Well, yes, that would be a good thing."

"And what about you, Rose?"

"We'll take any prayer we can get."

At this point Alleyne Zimmer spoke. "I could have got married at one stage; but I turned away from it. I felt I had done the right thing. I've always felt that way; yet there have been times when I've had my doubts. If this is right for you, Rose, then I wish you much happiness."

"I really appreciate that," Rose replied.

So the group prayed for Peter and Rose. He had not meant to go public, but somehow these prayers helped him to feel that they were really doing the right thing.

80

The meeting was going well, Arnold reflected. He was thrilled that Alleyne had asked for prayer, and he was very happy that Peter and Rose were becoming such good friends.

Nor was that the end of their intercessions. Tim mentioned a Chinese waiter with whom he had had good conversations at a restaurant he frequented. Big Lil requested prayer for her deliverance ministry, that she might get things right: this was a new feature, as in the past she always seemed to think that she was already getting things right. Sister Cecilia mentioned a nun at the convent who was drawing near to the end of her life, but who seemed strangely troubled.

In the end, only Arnold and Kathleen had not requested prayer.

"What about you?" Big Lil asked, looking at them expectantly. "How can we pray for you?"

He stole a glance at Kathleen and sensed from her that she would welcome some wise sharing. "We would like you to pray about our future," he said. "There are a number of reasons why it may be right for us to stay back home this time, even though we have a heart for the work here."

"You would be missed," Rose said.

"I expect the bookshop would continue, but with someone else looking after it. Even if we only went on furlough and came back again, there would still be need for a temporary replacement."

"What would you do?" Tim asked. "Things seem to be very tough in Northern Ireland at the moment."

"I know. It just seems to get worse, sure it does. Nothing's clear yet. If we stay, we may be in Northern Ireland or we may be in England. We've got roots in both."

"I could never leave my work here," Alleyne said, "unless I really had to."

"Yes," Rose responded. "We all know how dedicated you are. But God treats us all differently. We have to be sensitive to his call."

"Any special reason for not coming back?" Peter asked. "Something you'd like to share?"

"I don't think it would be wise to share," Arnold said, "but there are a few things coming together at this time."

"You would be able to go back into journalism," Tim said. "You're good at that."

"If they'll have me. Or God may have something quite different for us."

"That's right," said Big Lil. "We've got to be open to his will. If we are out of his will, we have a very disappointing life."

"So how should we pray?" Peter asked.

"Just as we have been saying – pray that we may be clear about whether we should come back or not; and if we stay over there that there may be a suitable job and peace about where we should live."

This was the signal for a further burst of prayer. By the time the others had finished praying, it was late enough to end the meeting. "That was a good meeting," Arnold declared. "And we were so happy to welcome Miss Zimmer."

"I never thought I would come here," Alleyne admitted, "but I'm glad that I did."

"We shall miss this meeting," Peter said. "It won't be the same when you've gone."

"Maybe they can meet at your house instead," Arnold suggested.

"It would be hard for me – for us – to match your hospitality." It was obvious that Peter was trying to choose his words carefully. So many of them were potentially on the cusp of change.

As they prepared to leave, Arnold said, "I wonder where we will all be in ten years' time."

Where indeed?

BOOK SIX : JULY 1982

81

Rose had been surprised at first to discover how hard it was to settle down to life in England again. When you went overseas you expected everything to be different, but nobody had prepared her for the shock of re-entry, when so many familiar goalposts had been removed.

As anticipated, the relationship between Peter and herself had prospered, but they had waited until furlough the following year so that they could get married with family members around them. Before the actual marriage, Rose had to apply to Peter's mission and be accepted by them. If they had refused her, there would have been a big dilemma. As Peter's parents had been reluctant to endure the extra burden of hosting them, they had stayed for the most part in Blackburn, despite the overcrowding. This had given her more time to spend also with her sister Ethel and her two children.

For their two tours of service together they had lived at the men's hostel, where she soon got to know the students. After working exclusively with female students, it was odd to be surrounded by so many males. However, she maintained some contact with the girls, and had seen Catherine return to her studies, and at a later stage become a pastor's wife.

Meanwhile at a Christian hospital in the centre of the country she had given birth to two daughters: Elaine was born in May

1974 and Suzanne two years later. The students were delighted to have two small children in their midst, and there was never any shortage of baby sitters.

She still remembered that day when she had first taken Elaine out in her pram and a church member had stopped to chat with her. When this lady discovered that the baby was only seven days old, she became alarmed and urged her to go home at once, since it was regarded as necessary in the local culture to keep a new-born baby inside for a month.

On their next furlough, she had taken great delight in showing the girls off to family and friends; and even Peter's family had warmed to these new arrivals.

Eventually it was time to think of their education. At first they started a little school at their home, and two other missionary children came to join in. Suzanne was really too young for proper schooling, but still insisted in joining the others. When others saw how she taught them, they suggested that she had missed her vocation.

Eventually, it was necessary to give more consideration to their future. If they were to stay on in Taiwan, the girls would have to go to a school in the centre of the country, where they would get a basically American education. There was also the question of Peter's work, for he felt it was time to move on from student ministry. When they discussed this with their mission bosses, they were asked if they would like to work back in the UK as area secretaries. That was why they now lived on the edge of Birmingham.

It was Sunday afternoon, and she had taken the girls to the park, where they enjoyed the swings. Peter was away at a church some thirty miles away, and would be back late that evening. That was the only problem with such a job: it meant that he was away from home rather more than both of them would have liked. The girls would keep asking when Daddy was coming back, and often she had to inform them that it would not be till they were in bed. She was not to be cajoled into letting them stay up late simply in order to see him, as that would make them too tired when they went to school the next day.

"Time to go home," she announced.

"Oh, Mummy, couldn't we stay a bit longer?" Elaine asked, but she decided she must be firm. As they began to walk home, both girls cast reluctant glances back at the joys behind them.

"When's Daddy coming back?" Elaine asked. She was the more dominant of the two, always asking questions, whereas Suzanne was content to let the world go by without too much fuss.

"He'll be back tonight."

"Can we stay up to see him?"

"Now, Elaine, you know the answer to that one. You'll see plenty of him tomorrow."

"But we'll be at school."

"Not all day. He will be there to read you stories."

"I wish he was here more often."

"And where would you be if Daddy was not around to earn the pennies to keep you alive?"

Children were great fun despite the hard work. In a way she felt sorry for Miss Price. Despite all her warnings, she had married late in life, but too old to have children. This had come as a great surprise to everyone who knew her, but she seemed happy enough.

The house was a bit small for Rose's family, and one room had to serve as a meeting room, but they got by. If they had gone straight into a parish, the size of the house might have been somewhat daunting. They had got involved with a local church, and Rose now found herself running a women's group. This was a welcome development, for so much of the current ministry went to Peter and not to herself. The ladies were eager to learn and they had also become good friends.

"Home again!" she announced.

"Can we have a biscuit?" Suzanne asked. She was the one with the bigger appetite.

"Let's get in first and then we'll take a look in the biscuit tin."

Her mother would be coming for a visit in a week's time and that was always something to look forward to. She still missed her father, but she could only look back on family times with affection. The girls were very fond of their nana.

It had been a happy life up to this point, and she had every reason to believe that it would continue to be.

82

As she walked up the garden path, having enjoyed her walk in the park with her dog Billy, Alleyne paused to look at the roses. They were coming on well this year. She opened the door, walked down the hall to the kitchen, set down the bags and filled a bowl with water for the dog.

She had never imagined it would be so easy to settle into American life. It had taken a bit of time, but eventually the mission had been able to provide a job in this city and to rent an apartment for her use. At first it was not easy to get involved in the student scene, but she had persevered and, before long, a little group of students from Taiwan, mainly girls, came to meet at her place for fellowship. In this setting her age was an advantage, as the Chinese have a great respect for older people.

When her time of working for the mission was over, she asked if she could continue this work on a voluntary basis, and the mission encouraged her to do so. There was even some assistance with her rent. Now she could not see herself giving up this ministry, unless she became too old or decrepit to handle it.

Soon it was as if this little group of students had known each other for years. Although she had tried to maintain good relationships with the students at the seminary in Taiwan, it was so much easier to get alongside these overseas students. It was a joy that so many of them came from Mainland China. Maybe that was largely because she had mellowed. Ever since the death of her friend Helen and the strength she had derived from Christian friends to help her through it, she had been a different person – less judgmental and more adaptable.

The mission had started similar work in other cities, and Alleyne would go to meet the new workers and give them encouragement. Although she was officially retired, she delighted in any opportunities she still had for ministry.

Even living in a Western environment was easier for her than she had anticipated. She had gained a number of friends; but she was still most at home when she was in the company of Chinese visitors. This pleased her, for she had much more to give than those who had worked only on American soil.

Yesterday she had received a letter from Rose. Sometimes when she looked back she regretted the coldness of her attitude to Rose over several years; and yet that terrible incident had changed everything. Now they were able to exchange letters as if they had always been on good terms. She had missed such a lot during those long years of unsociability. Of course, at the time, she had not thought there was anything wrong: it was only with hindsight that she had become aware of her shortcomings.

A week earlier the former principal of the seminary had come to visit her, as he was on a visit to the States. She appreciated his taking the time and trouble to seek her out. Now they could laugh and reminisce together. How different from those formal and uneasy conversations in his study! He told her that life at the seminary was good and that there were more students than ever. Although he was now in an administrative job at a church headquarters, he liked to keep up with the place where he had spent so many years.

When she had enjoyed a cup of tea and dozed over a devotional book, she set out cookies for the evening visitors and boiled a kettle.

Grace was the first to arrive. "Miss Zimmer!" she called as she came over the threshold beaming. "I've got so many things to tell you." How good it was that they took her so much into their confidence.

Diana came with a basket of fruit. "I have brought this for you," she said. "You are always so kind to us."

Sarah was the next to arrive. "When I come here," she said, "it is like being home in Taiwan."

Alleyne recalled the letter she had received a few days ago from Merlin Katz. This had led her to consider what might have been. She could have had a family of her own; and yet, she reflected, in a sense, she had her own family already.

83

It was always a struggle for Peter to stay fresh in his deputation ministry. There were certain things which had to be said over and over again. When he was preaching, however, he always produced a new sermon, even if many of the real-life examples had been given before. At some churches it was a real joy to speak, for he knew that there was a thriving interest in the work of the mission; but in other churches he was less confident, as it was likely his words would bear little influence when it came to ongoing support. However, he treated all with equal courtesy in his travels.

This was one of the stronger supporting churches. As an Anglican he had no problem with speaking in a Baptist church. Had not his missionary experience taught him to enjoy Christian fellowship wherever he could find it.? After the evening service there was a further meeting at which he was asked to speak a little more briefly and to show a few slides. After this, others lingered to talk with him. Although he was longing to get back home, he gave them all the time they sought, and when he got into his car he was satisfied that this was a job well done.

Fortunately, it would take only about three quarters of an hour to get home. Those two terms of service together in Taiwan had been very happy ones. They had both been sorry to leave, but there were so many factors indicating that this was the right thing to do.

It was always good to hear from his former students. Simon had become a Presbyterian minister and was now pastoring a church in the capital. It was so encouraging to see one of his converts working full time for the Lord.

Paul's girl friend had recovered well, and when Paul, on

graduation, had completed his military service, they had married, and recently they had moved to New York. Peter still did not know what kind of work he was doing there, but was determined to find out.

He got Christmas messages each year from the Earwicker family. Relations between Craig and his parents did not seem to have improved, but, as he was now at college in Baltimore, they did not rub shoulders regularly, and he seemed to be carving out a meaningful life for himself.

Geoffrey had married an old school friend and they had recently moved with their son and daughter to Wolverhampton, which was not far away from his own home. Thus they were able to exchange visits from time to time. He could see that Geoffrey's home was just as inviting and hospitable as his parents' had always been. He hoped his own home could be regarded in the same way.

It was hard to recall those old bachelor days. For him now, life would have been meaningless without having Rose there in the middle of it. Sometimes it irked him that he had to travel so much, but when he was back home with the family they always made up for lost time. He hoped that Rose would not feel underemployed, since she had no viable work of her own, except for responsibility for the ladies' group; but she seemed to enjoy her work with them, and, when it was possible, they would take meetings together.

At last he was driving up that familiar street where he lived. He parked in the driveway of the house. Even before he got to the door, it was opened and Rose was standing there radiant with welcome. They exchanged a long hug. How could his parents have been content without such demonstrations of love and togetherness? In his family they would all take as many hugs as they could get.

"Do you want help unloading the car?" Rose asked.

"You can take some of the lighter things."

It only took a few moments to empty the car of its contents. The door closed behind them

84

As the book signing did not begin till 11, Arnold had plenty of time to walk from his home to the bookstore. He had been allowed a day off work for this purpose.

At first it had been difficult to get a job; but eventually, with the help of a friend, he had landed this job as a journalist in Milton Keynes. His old skills soon came back and, apart from the geographical surroundings, it was as if he had never been away from the job. He felt very much at home. It was not too far either for Kathleen to go if she wanted to see her relatives. Good schools too had been found for the boys.

Philip at 15 was a keen sportsman, whose main claim to fame was that he could run very fast. Sammy, now known as Sam, at 13 was a little more academic, but was also a fun-loving character. It was such a delight to watch their progress. Now that the boys were older, Kathleen worked part-time in a cake shop. She enjoyed this opportunity to mix with others.

He still missed Taiwan. Life had seemed flat for a while after their return. Although he still maintained contact with a few friends, it was not the same as actually being with them. He had tried to find out what had happened to Frank, but nobody had any news of him. He feared the worst, but there was no way in which he could know for sure what had happened. One of the staff members at the college, he heard, had been refused a visa to return after furlough: that could well have been his own fate. They had found someone else to run the shop, but after three years it had closed. Now there was nobody to take the good news out into the villages.

It had come as a complete surprise when Dick had approached him. They had only met once, and that briefly, at Sun Moon Lake when the older man was due to retire. Despite his advancing years, the retired missionary had a strong desire to tell his life story so that others could learn from his experiences and he had not forgotten that brief encounter. When approached, he had first been surprised, but he soon warmed to the idea. As Dick Spurling lived only ten miles away, they had been able to meet up frequently. At last, he had written a first draft. Dick had looked at it and suggested some changes.

Now, at last, the book was published, and was made available in Christian bookshops. Dick would be with him at the local shop today to sign copies.

This was for him a new venture, but one for which he felt the Lord had prepared him; for he was not just a journalist but a man with experience of Christian work in the Far East.

Although Dick had done very different work from Arnold's, much of his experience was an echo of his. At last Arnold had a sense not just of being called back into something that had formerly been a big part of his life, but of being called forward into something new. If this book were well received, he might even write others.

Sometimes he regretted not moving back to Northern Ireland, especially as so many of his friends and relatives there were going through such difficult times. If a job had opened itself to him there, he would probably have taken it. But he had also had to take into account Kathleen's timidity after that incident with Sammy: living in such a situation she might have become fearful for the lives of both her sons. He had had to content himself with a number of visits, and he had reported on Irish incidents in the local newspaper when they were big enough to command attention. One day, he hoped, there would be some successful agreement for a peaceful future, but it still seemed a long way off.

Here was the shop, and Dick was standing in the doorway to receive him.

"I wonder if anyone will come," Dick remarked.

"They will," Arnold assured him. "I think there will be a lot of interest in your story. I found it fascinating."

They went in, and were escorted to a desk piled high with copies of the book. Already there was a little queue of people waiting to have their books signed. Dick's face lit up.

"Here are two seats for you, gentlemen," said the proprietress. "Start whenever you are ready."

This shop seemed so much bigger than the one in Taiwan. In a way his life had come full circle.

46010717R00182

Made in the USA
Charleston, SC
09 September 2015